I0680409

Jay Rani

Courtesan and a Psychoanalyst
New York Love Story

KGB agent: Mr. Hemingway—
Et tu Brute, Erneste?
Rhymed Essay

Free Kisses
From Prague, Paris, Pamplona, Brazil,
and NY with Harlem
Rhymed Stories and Frivolous Poems

2010

Text copyright © Jay Rani, 2010
www.jayrani.com
Šafaříková 455/7, Prague, 120 00
Czech Republic

Courtesan and a Psychoanalyst
Free Kisses

Cover page and the illustrations concepts by Jay Rani.
Photography by Julia Novitskaja.
Cover girl—Cassandra (Miss. Gabriela Kloudová).
Illustrations were drawn by T. M. Larsen.

Book and eBook design by Kvakes
www.kvakes.com

ISBN 978-80-254-7574-4

To the Girls I loved

Author acknowledges editorial
and inspirational contributions by:
Jana Svobodová, PhDr.—writer,
Marek Polanecký—poet,
Katerina Konečna, M.A.—linguist,
Jason Smolek and David Papiasvili—consultations
in English and proofreading,
Vladimir Osif—Parisian painter.

Inspirational and logistic support was provided
by chorus line of lovely young ladies:
Cassandra, Alina Abramova, Petra Váňová, Slavia
Bert, Ingrid Gillming and others who did not wish
to disclose their names.

Preface

Fasten your seatbelts, the sea is waking-up, and the wind starts blowing.

The first meeting with Jay Rani was literally like a dream for me. I woke up from it after two days with a liver-ache. Subsequently, I wondered who is hiding behind the face of a rebel that reminded me of Allen Ginsberg and Gregory Corso. So, it was no surprise to me when I found out that he had been writing poetry since the age of seventeen. First, he wrote in Georgian then in Russian and later switched to English... but let me rather go back to his origins.

Jay Rani (Avtandil Alex Papiasvili) was born and raised in Georgia. Later, he graduated from a medical school in Soviet Russia. He completed his psychiatric training in communist Czechoslovakia and afterwards "escaped" from behind the Iron Curtain, to the USA. From his early days as a young doctor in the Sovi et Union, he was discreetly gathering documents incriminating the KGB in the misuse of psychiatry against the political dissent. After his escape, he presented the documents to Pavel Tigrid (leader of the Czech political emigration in Paris), who published them in his magazine "Testimony". Jay Rani also presented his materials at a press conference in London (August 31, 1977). Consequently, the World Psychiatric Association has issued an official condemnation of the Soviets practices.

He settled in New York, where he worked as a medical doctor—psychiatrist. J. Amirani later taught at Cornell University Medical College and published several scientific studies. He also had his own live TV show about sexology in New York (RTVI Channel).

Throughout all these years, he continued his creative work in literature—poems, stories, and plays. This was the place where he felt happiest.

A few years ago, he returned to Czech Republic where he lives as a cosmopolitan writer between New York and Prague. His time has finally come—Jay Rani has decided to publish his collected literary works.

I wish you a pleasant reading and I believe that his short novel and rhymed stories will bring you the same joy and pleasure as they brought to me.

Now, please, fasten your seatbelts...

Marek Polanecký,
poet and radio anchorman

Contents

Mellow Wine is the Most Sparkling   9
Foreword by Jana Svobodová, Ph.D., writer

Courtesan and a Psychoanalyst   11
New York Love Story

**KGB Agent: Mr. Hemingway—
Et Tu Brute, Erneste?**   77
Rhymed Essay

Free Kisses   83
Rhymed Stories and Frivolous Poems

I. From Prague, Paris, Spain and Brazil

To Muse   87
The Elegant Lily   89
Don't Leave Me Now   93
In Paris—with the Drifter Girls   95
Return to Montmartre—
    to the Home Gone   97
Under the Montmartre Stars   99
Lousy Rainy Night in Paris' Streets   101
Dirty Dancer   105
Somewhere in Brazil   109
Love in a Rio Pub   114
The Bullfight Ring   117
Who Said Hemingway Loved
    the Bullfights   119

II. From New York

Free Kisses in the Big Apple 123
She Was Only a Girl 127
Sex for Shelter 131
On NYC Racetrack 148
Wendy, Curly and Leggy 152
Looking for a Place in New York 157
To Our Sons 159
"People"—a Bunch
   of Frightened Individuals 160

III. From Harlem

Be Strong or Die in Harlem 165
$2 Deals in the Harlem Streets 176
Nightly Harlem 180
Harlem Riots 181
Blond Courtesan in a Harlem Club 185

Georgian poem "Farewell"

In Georgian script 193
English translation 194

About My Writings

About My Writings 195

Mellow Wine is the Most Sparkling

"Mellow wine is the most sparkling"—I was once told. We can say the same about poetry and a novelette by Jay Rani (Avtandil Alex Papiasvili).

Born in Republic of Georgia, he spent his childhood in the USSR behind the Iron Curtain. He finished his medico—psychiatric trainings at university in the Czechoslovak town of Brno. Only when he could no longer stand the oppressions of the communist regime in Russian occupied Czechoslovakia (after August 21, 1968) he daringly escaped through the "Iron Curtain" obtaining the political asylum in the USA. He finally settled in New York City.

Quite soon, however, he was awaken by the place, where he had landed in his almost Ahasuerian journey. Therefore, he lets one of his heroes express the opinion that everybody is a puppet of an establishment, which is pushing and forcing them to subdue to the written and unwritten rules of political and social correctness. His manly and sensitive (but never sentimental) poetry and his novelette "Courtesan and a Psychoanalyst" express his rich life experience. They express his true sympathy and empathy for all human weaknesses and faults, while at the same time he is sharply critical to any kind of societies, where "the poor stay poor and the rich get rich" (quoted from his admired Leonard Cohen verses).

Throughout all his fruitful life, he nursed his youth's dream—to become a poet, a novelist, a published author, who has much to say to his readers. However, only in the last few years he has found conditions to make his dream come true.

Amirani's poetry and prose flashes a remarkable gift for writing, where the brighter, as well as the darker sides are spiced and peppered-up with both sharp and indulgent hearty humor.

Well, we can only expect a new work from the author and hope that it will find its way to the readers very, very soon.

Jana Svobodová, Ph. D.,
writer, author of "Life of the Emperors"

Courtesan and a Psychoanalyst

New York Love Story

I

Any reasonably sane New Yorker knows that when we talk about Manhattan's Upper East Side or Westchester County, we are talking about an upper middle class luxurious lifestyle. We are talking about good citizens who make their money mostly by legal means, and even pay their taxes, mostly through honest ways.

Doctor J. was a Westchester county resident who drove daily his reasonably luxury car to the Manhattan office. Although his official, politically correct title was psychoanalyst, he liked to call himself a shrink; it was New York City after all. Despite this, he was a recognized M.D., psychiatrist, and psychoanalyst. Everyone in his surroundings, including his patients and himself, knew the importance of this three-step gradation. The best schools and proper trainings were behind him and he had a glitzy office address, to match—on Manhattan's Upper East Side.

Even his name was appropriate for his status—Jeffrey Glassman, M.D. His friends from residency training, however, called him simply Doctor J.

His patients came from the same proper social strata—all were upper middle class and good citizens like him. Dr. J., with his roots in Westchester County and a prestigious university position of Assistant Professor, had a real chance to advance his career. He was up for promotion—appointment as an Associate Professor and a Training Analyst in the University Psychoanalytic Institute where he presently taught. It was the place where he had spent his student years.

* * *

Katie was an out of town girl, from Virginia. Her business was in the realm of men's psychological counseling and physical stress reduction—or so she claimed.

That was a care for all men who could afford that kind of care for cash.

It was not an easy business for a new girl in the city. Even for a girl with her street smarts, good looks, and leggy-legs.

Katie used to call herself a puppet of society—"We are all just puppets in our own social surroundings and in society at large," she often said. There were unwritten rules of correctness and Katie was highly aware of them. "There are those who were born rightly and those who were not so lucky. Therefore, those who *were not* can only count on themselves to make it in this world." This was Katie's life-philosophy.

Katie's talent was her ability to address the psychological needs of men—to discover their innermost desires. The desires so unspeakable that most could not even admit it to themselves. The official society, alias Establishment recognized two types of desires—Politically Correct, and those Politically Incorrect; all proper men had difficulties admitting to those incorrect ones. When she understood the depth of a man's real wish, she knew how to play as the kind of woman who would satisfy him. She played the psychosexual games with such intensity that often she herself achieved an orgasm, even though it was not necessarily her aim.

She was also an exhibitionist and a born manipulator; she knew what kind of perfume, and what kind of dress to wear to drive men to the edge. Her instinct told her where to go bra-less in a mini skirt with high heels, like a whore, and where to wear a black long dress like a lady. She knew, men would wonder what she was wearing underneath, if anything. These were her prospective clients. Men pay more for the tease, foreplay and role-play than for intercourse itself.

Katie has been conducting business in her luxury Upper East Side three-bedroom apartment. She was a proficient businesswoman and there was never a dull moment in her place. She employed two girls so three clients could be serviced at the same time. Katie never called herself a madam since she saw the entire training as a Sex therapy program. She had particular interest in men presenting themselves as sexual giants but failing in bed. It took some time for them to realize that it was not the girl, but their Ego trip that was to blame. Only then, she could do something with them; well, assuming the client kept his appointments and did not switch to another sex establishment.

Men with middle age crises were the most problematic. Seeing their marriages gone wrong or gone as such, they have to deal now with declining sexuality. To make things even worse, they would wait too long before coming for advice. They came only after they stopped having sex and started to worry about their prostates.

She felt overworked sometimes, but on the other hand, the more she worked, the more she felt alive. This was the other side of the coin—the brighter side.

Katie particularly enjoyed curious cases. Once she saw this guy sitting on the corridor floor near her apartment. He broke her heart—so cute, and all drenched from a rainstorm. His name was Joshua. He was a stockbroker. His analyst had an office next door, and Joshua, being an early first patient, awaited his analyst's arrival. Katie invited him inside to dry out a little and have coffee. He sat there talking to Katie until his psychoanalyst opened the office. At first, he looked at her as a Goddess, but soon she noticed plain sexual desire in his eyes.

Next time he came for coffee he already understood what this place was about and accepted an offer—having sex-for-pay just before his psychoanalytic therapy session. Katie set the start-up fee and assigned him to Olga—a nice and sensible Russian girl.

Joshua never missed an appointment and soon his eyes began to open. He made more eye contact while conversing and cracked a sarcastic joke. Olga said he was quite good in bed. He loved his wife, but wished his wife would be as sexy as Olga would. Katie instructed Olga to work with him more sensually, so he could inspire his wife to be the same.

Once he told Katie that he did not know how to tell his analyst about all this. That the analyst was noticing the change in his behavior and Joshua felt like a coward hiding *this* from him. Katie replied there was no way around it and eventually he would have to disclose it. What was there to be afraid of after all? What could possibly happen so terrible to him!

* * *

Doctor Glassman had been deeply convinced that only the M.D. psychiatrists like him could make real psychoanalysts. There was fundamental difference between him, as an M.D. psychiatrist, and many psychologists who also called themselves psycho-analysts. Moreover, the plain New Yorkers called all of them simply the therapists, the Shrinks, and even the Shamans—adding insult to the injury.

One could only imagine Dr. J's demeanor when his mother in law, at a family dinner, asked him, what the difference between a psychiatrist and a psychologist was. Jeffrey Glassman, M.D. would excuse himself to the bathroom, so he could curse without anybody hearing him.

His own fifteen year-old marriage was in fine shape—at least no worse than any of his colleagues, as far as he knew. His wife Rebecca believed there was no need to dwell on timeless quest for perfect sexual satisfaction. She was an intellectual and a very busy person for such thoughts. So, all was fine between them—an upper middle class family with their two kids placed in upscale Westchester schools.

It is not that he never had unwanted feelings and thoughts. Those would usually overwhelm him when he saw beautiful young girls in the short micro-mini skirts and high heels. Their hemlines slipping to high, accidentally showing stocking tops with white flesh. The student-girls used to do it in the university classrooms where he would teach seminars to small groups. He would even get a glimpse at their panties under the skirts, and would then suspect that they flashed him deliberately—

just to tantalize their proper professor. Therefore, he strictly held up to his professional conduct and kept his gaze forward, to the boys, and away from the girls. Sometimes though, the sexual excitement would painfully overwhelm him and he had difficulties with concentrating on his work.

He did not consider masturbation a sickness or damaging to one's health, but regarded it as an inferior way of sexual satisfaction ... and sign of Ego weakness. After all, he was married, and had a "healthy" sex-life with his wife.

They had sex once a week on average—a normal frequency by his medical books. He was the one who always initiated sex, and even softly "insisted" on it. Rebecca, who was in her late forties, did not actively seek sexual acts—she was more interested in the children and her own career. They made love usually in missionary position, with lights off; she turned to the other side and slept right after "it was over". This was their Politically Correct sex. He knew he could not demand more sex from his wife—that would be illegal according to American laws, since it could be interpreted as a "marital rape", in legal terms.

Jeffrey unfortunately had difficulties to fall asleep after this kind of sex; he dreamt about the student girls in micro-minis. He particularly dreamt about them when his wife, for "understandable reasons", would refuse sex with him. Those nights he not only dreamt, but also vividly felt the student girls ... He saw them not only in micro-minis, but also in erotic lingerie ... And there was no way to stop it! Engulfed by his uncontrollable pleasure, and accompanied by humiliation he masturbated right in the bed, lying next to his wife. These were nights of his psychological battles, the battles of his willpower, which he invariably lost on the heights of overwhelming pleasure.

He could probably go to the bathroom to do it, but he probably, subconsciously, wished to be caught by his wife. Maybe then, she would understand that Jeffrey, as a middle-aged man probably needs more sex, than she does, as a woman of same age. Maybe she would then become more accommodating to his sexual needs ...

They would sit in the morning with Rebecca, drink coffee, eat breakfast, and pretend that all was fine between them. Jeffrey hoped she did not notice anything ... or maybe she did know all, but preferred to not to talk—just to shovel it under the rug instead. Evidently, this intelligent, well-cultured woman would rather see her husband go to prostitutes, than be more sexually accommodative to him. Perhaps she was brought up this way.

Jeffrey felt shame and guilt for his weakness and it came to his mind that perhaps he should find a younger lover or at least a prostitute, so he would stop doing "this".

Jeffrey Glassman, M.D. was not giving up, however. He went back to his old psychoanalyst to discuss and analyze his compulsions. Sometimes he even took a sleeping pill for calming himself down. This was rare, very rare, and always without anyone's knowledge—not even his psychoanalyst. He knew the best medicine was just to take his mind off it and put his energy into sports and other extracurricular activities. To take the kids to soccer games, to get involved with community affairs, to volunteer for senior citizens clubs, etc, etc. ... and, certainly not to look at young girls in the classroom or at soccer games. He was really doing his best and believed in a final victory over his (overwhelmingly pleasurable) weakness. He simply knew—one day he would stop masturbating.

"That is enough,"—he thought,—"too many thoughts are leading to more obsessions". There was a psychoanalytic conference coming up and he was a keynote speaker. He needed to prepare his speech.

He tried to live his life through the science and art of psychoanalysis. He also lived it through his patients and often noted that both he and his patients went through the same kind of problems and resolutions. Mysteriously, the same things were happening in both his and his patients' lives at the same time. It is like there was an invisible Thread connecting their mental processes. He knew this was called a "counter transference", "parallel process", and other smart names, but main thing was that Tread worked only when there was a good therapeutic relationship. These were things inexplicable by scientific means and he would tell to his students and supervises— "Do not try to explain everything—leave something to the magic. Do not dig too deep into the patient's unconscious; you may uncover more than you can handle." He was well liked and respected by them.

* * *

Joshua Bauman was Dr. J's patient. His difficulty was in his vagueness. He was an accomplished stockbroker, but had constant difficulties expressing his feelings and thoughts. His relationship with his wife was not going well either. His sex life was so-so and he was not sure if he wanted children with her or not. He was not making progress in therapy either. Dr. J. knew that this vagueness might go on for years before the psychoanalytic process would bring any change.

However, Dr. J. noticed that Joshua's behavior had unexpectedly changed at some point. He had become more secretive and clearly had something to say but could not break the ice. One day it happened by itself ..., and here was Joshua with his eyes wide open telling his story, telling it as if challenging the analyst. Joshua has been having an affair and felt satisfied with whatever what was going on.

Here was Joshua's story: Dr. J. had his office in a large residential building in a rented apartment. Joshua always came for the first session in the early morning. Dr. J. had no receptionist or any other kind of staff and always opened the office himself just 15 minutes before the start of the first session. Joshua, however, would come about an hour before his session, sit on the floor of the corridor next to his office, and read The New York Times. That is where he met somebody.

"She is a counselor and has an office on the same floor as you," he explained to Dr. J. with a challenging, and almost aggressive streak in his voice. He was sure the doctor is going to disapprove and even throw him out of his office for the immorality. Dr. J. just sat there in amazement. This counselor of Joshua seemed to be one of those pseudo-therapists proclaiming they could treat anything. Therefore, he asked what the therapist was treating.

"No, she does not treat anything," —said Joshua— "She just helps you to deal with your sexuality— provides sexual service."

"How does she help you with your sexuality and how much does she charge for this service?" Dr. J. could not think of anything better.

"The fee is important of course, as everywhere. Her fee is 250 dollars for a one hour full service session." The fee was just about the same as Dr. J's fee for psychoanalysis, but his sessions were 45 min. only—not a full hour.

"What does the Full Service mean, if I may know?"

"It means full sexual intercourse"—Joshua paused—"Just plain, normal sex."

Joshua looked like a real winner as he made firm eye contact with Jeffrey Glassman, M.D. His eyes said, "I'm not afraid of you." This was the first time he dared to confront his psychiatrist whom he always saw as an authority figure. The Doctor himself was little startled. It was clear—sex sessions were more important to Joshua than psychoanalysis. Dr. J. realized that the patient might really act out and leave the treatment if he tried to stop his sex sessions. The power struggle could be destructive.

"Well, having an extramarital affair is not something legally prohibited. It all depends whether we can talk about it or not." Dr. J. was realizing that his heartbeat was up. It was important to stay in charge of the situation.

"You mean its ok with you that I am having paid sex before coming to your office for psychoanalysis?" Joshua looked surprised.

"Whatever you do outside of this office is your own business. As far as having extramarital sex on the same floor is concerned, there is little difference whether you have it next door or somewhere in the city. It is fine as long as we can discuss your feelings here." Joshua could not believe it.

"So, I may continue visiting both—sex for pay and psychoanalysis, for pay as well, next door from each other?

"Do you want to talk about it now?" Jeffrey Glassman, M.D. felt like he was back in control again.

*   *   *

One morning Katie found a business card stuck in her door. The business card, belonging to Jeffrey Glassman, M.D., psychoanalyst, asked her to call his office at a suitable time. The address on the card was notable—it was the same building as hers, even the same floor. She realized this was Joshua's analyst and called him to set a meeting. She saw him several times in the building and even spoke on a few occasions. It happened when they both were picking up their mail in the lobby and bumped into one another. They then exchanged a few words and awkward smiles, but this was not what touched her. It was his smell; the smell of an intelligent, well bred, and cultivated man who was born for high society. The aroma she never smelled before so intensely.

Days before the meeting she experienced strange feelings. On one hand, she was looking forward to see him, but on the other, she felt anxious and even "afraid" of this meeting. She never felt anything like this ... at least not for long. This was something she always believed was easy to handle for her ... but now ... or maybe she was just imagining all and behaving like a little girl, like when she played "Mom and Dad" with her dolls.

They met on Monday, during a "window hour" they both had in-between sessions. Katie called and Dr. J. suggested meeting in his office for about twenty minutes.

Dr. J. opened the door and realized he has already seen and spoken to her on occasion. Katie was dressed in a business suit with tiny slits on both sides of her skirt. She was wearing black heels with sheer stockings and her cleavage was just deep enough to attract the hidden glances of the doctor.

Dr. J. was in his regular psychiatrist uniform, as he called it—a grey three-piece suit with tie and black (not brown) shoes.

"Katherine Johns"—she said, making strong and charming eye contact.

"Doctor Glassman"—he said in low voice—"Please, sit down, I suppose you know why I asked you to meet."

"I suppose it's about Joshua."

"Is it true that ... that he's been coming to your apartment to have ... " Dr. J. trailed off.

"To have sex ..." Katie finished for him—"Sex and relaxation for a fee. You can also call it stress reduction with a surrogate sex therapist"—Katie felt tension and caught herself getting defensive.

Dr. J. had to catch his breath before he could open his mouth.

"Those are big words. I would not call it therapy ... but at this point, I am just concerned about the well-being of my patient. Are you aware of the potential harm this ... paid sex could bring to him?"—He almost saw his own face with his eyes hiding behind his glasses.

"Yes, I am aware that this is a very delicate matter which needs a very sensitive approach. A wrong move could cause harm as, for example, when a surgeon operates on the brain. Even the smallest wrong move could be fatal."—She still could not relax and Dr. J. was not helping.

He paused for a while. They both sat in silence, looking at each other as if studying any tiny body movements. He forced himself to look away from her breasts. There was a birthmark on the lower part of her ivory white neck. Suddenly he became aware of her perfume, he had smelled the odor from the beginning, but was not aware of it until now.

"Did you at least ask about his health condition or if he was taking any medications?"—He nearly squeezed the words out of his mouth speaking in a conciliatory tone.

"Of course, after all I am a psychologist."

"You are a psychologist?"—Dr. J. moved in his chair.

"Just masters level, not a Ph.D."

"... What on the earth made you to do *this*? Did your parents abuse you or something? Sorry for asking ..."

"No, that's OK, it's not the first time I hear it. I just like this lifestyle since my college days. It is good for men too."—Katie had a feeling she was talking too much, almost lecturing—"After all Courtesans and Geishas had been around since the dawn of civilization."—Katie ended her speech, feeling as though she were standing in front of her professor or a judge.

Dr. J. had hard time listening, however. He secretly concentrated on her body language, noticing her knees with the skirt riding higher up to her thighs and her sheer blouse with the silhouette of the bra through her open jacket.

"Is Joshua having ... this ... with ... you?"

"No, he is not having "this" with me. He is having it with my assistant."—answered she in fact and smiled.

"Well, I hope we're both primarily concerned about Joshua's psychological and ... sexual health."—He said finally.

"I will most definitely consult you should the need arise."

"Make sure you have the patient's consent."—Dr. J. ended the conversation. Katie still had something to say, but understood that her audience has ended. He ended it like an M.D., a psychiatrist and an older one by age, after all.

Dr. J. noticed again Katie's birthmark on her white neck. It was larger than he first thought. Dr. J. looked at the small clock on his desk. Their time was up—he thought. They actually spent 27 minutes talking. She got up to leave. He walked her to the door.

"Your birthmark, it could be dangerous. Do you have any more of those?"

"Yes, but they're all in such places that I couldn't possibly show you."—Katie could not believe that she said that, but the words were out and now she could only stare at his expression. She felt like a little girl who had just said something shameful and was waiting for daddy's reaction. Dr. J. paused for a second and decided to disregard the comment.

"Call me if you have any pertinent questions."— He said, closing the door and feeling in control again. Being in control was very important to him, but this time it was not the same. He had to stop and compose himself. He had a feeling he would see her again. Her "business" is her problem, he thought. A patient's care is most important after all. He also felt that he was justifying himself.

* * *

Joshua Bauman had a problem. His wife was not responding to him sexually. More precisely, she was not responding to his new attempts to excite her.

Olga kept prompting him to uncover what she enjoys during sex, what "does the trick" for her.

"Be more attentive to her. Study her body language. What is her favorite smell? What makes her smile? You know, if you can make a women laugh you can do anything to her. See if she smiles at your jokes, if she looks forward to be with you alone."

Joshua would listen in silence and Olga would smile and gently touch his cheek.

"Try not to think of her as your wife, but rather your secret lover. Try to make love to her the way she likes it. Discover her sexual fantasy."

Once Olga asked him after the sex:

"Do you ever fall asleep after making love during the day? It's a good indicator for a healthy sexual relationship."

Joshua had to think before answering.

"We never make love in the daytime or with any light at all."

* * *

Dr. J. had not seen Katie for a month since their talk in his office and was trying not to think about her. Joshua came regularly for his sessions and continued to improve.

Dr. J. met her again in the elevator. They were alone and both felt a little uncomfortable. The elevator took an awful long time. Dr. J. finally broke the ice.

"Is Joshua doing well?"—He did not really expect any serious answer, but Katie took it as a hint. "Perhaps we could talk about it over coffee at my place."—She gave him her card, looking at him with her big blue eyes that were now smiling mischievously. The elevator door finally opened and he realized that her scent was doing a trick on him. She walked into the lobby. His gaze secretly followed her skirt, slightly pleated at the hemline that swayed and moved with her hips as she walked toward the door. Dr. J. could not see her panty line through the fabric of the skirt. Was she wearing any? Or maybe she was just wearing a G-string? He had this compulsive image of her in a shorter skirt that would flash her garter belt hooks and stocking tops, if she moved quickly or bent over.

II

It was members only night at the men's club near Virginia Beach. All very serious middle-and-older aged men met to discuss club matters away from both public and family eyes. The clubhouse was built in a half circle around a courtyard with a swimming pool in the middle, with the beach within walking distance.

The club members started to arrive for early evening socializing. The only women were the service staff, including cocktail waitresses dressed as French Maids and the "entertainers." Their supervisor, Toni knew all the girls personally and was well-trusted by the club members.

Cocktail hour was followed by dinner and a discussion of club matters. The service staff endeavored to make the service perfect. Members ate and drank in anticipation of the entertainment.

There was a live jazz band followed by an obscure illusionist who did some common magic tricks for their amusement. The lights dimmed as the illusionist finished and the girls entered the room. The girls looked like models and were dressed as Playboy Easter Bunnies. They swung their bodies to the rhythm of music, inviting men to the dance floor. The girls danced a slow dance with the men that had joined them—a very slow dance. Some couples went back to the tables to continuing drinking and chatting. Other couples disappeared in the darkness, going to one of many different corners of the huge house. As more alcohol was consumed, more couples disappeared until there was only one lonesome man left sitting in a corner. He sat in the semi-dark room, nursing his drink and smoking a cigar.

There was a maid girl walking nearby. She approached the gentleman from the side so that he would see her, but think she had not noticed his gaze. She stared at something on the floor and bent over offering her round bottom for the gentleman's clear view. She was wearing a French Maid black miniskirt with white lace and black stockings with the seam up the back. The hooks of her garter belt were clearly visible. The white skin of her thighs flashed between the stocking tops and skirt hemline. She ignored the man's intense, almost mesmerized look and bent over even more as if picking something up from the floor. She straightened up and went on fixing her stockings standing several inches from the man. She raised the skirt so high that her white panties and red garter belt were fully exposed.

He made a somnambular movement as if reaching to touch her. She looked at him and walked slowly toward a small service room. She stopped, turned around to make sure that he was following, and entered the room with him. The door closed firmly behind them, giving the appearance that there was no one around.

One man watched them entering the small room, however, and that was Toni. He walked around a corner and approached the room from the other side where the door was ajar. The gentleman was in the frenzy of lovemaking, so much so that the scene looked picture-perfect even for Toni's experienced eyes. He watched them with the sudden surge of sexual arousal and pleasure of a voyeur. He knew he should get angry with the girl, as she was not supposed to be doing this: not while being on the service staff as a maid. There were different girls for this at the party—the entertainment crew. The minutes of their mating lasted forever with the girl moaning and wildly bucking her hips to meet his thrusts. Finally, it ended with him making a wild sound and she then turned around, fixing her panties and skirt. The gentleman handed her a couple of bills and the girl kissed him on the lips giving him a piece of paper.

"That's her phone number"—thought Toni and slowly entered the room. She was now alone there. Toni was clearly sexually aroused.

"You do know that you broke the rules and will be fired!"—Exclaimed Toni at her—"What is your name?"

"My name is Scarlet and I know I am taking business from the other girls." —She approached Toni slowly, keeping her sexy-wet gaze straight at his hungry eyes. She smiled with her natural sexy smile and said:

"But I could take care of you too..."

Aware of the aroma engulfing and paralyzing him Toni did not say anything. His eyes closed as by themselves for a second... He quickly opened them again. She was still keeping that sexy-wet gaze while straightening the skirt and fixing her hair. Smelling of sex, perfume and her own girly scent, she gave him a deep, open mouth kiss...and then one more, a tiny kiss on his cheek. Scarlet left the room without a word and Toni stood there a while taken aback. Nevertheless, she knew he would want to see her again.

Scarlet had learned how to turn tricks to make ends meet while still in graduate school. She also knew, that she loved the ambiance of promiscuity and would do the sex part even free, if she did not need the money. Scarlet just felt she was made to please both a man and herself alike. She was a natural Sexgem, ready for the oldest known profession.

The girls called her up the next day and said Toni wanted to see her. "Yes! I'm in!" she thought. It was an escort service where she got a slot for 3-4 days a week.

She could continue studying at the college and could quit her stupid night-waitress job at the local diner. Most importantly, Toni took a liking of her and invited her to the private club parties. This time she was part of the entertainment crew and was allowed to seduce and have sex with men at the parties. She was paid by Toni for those parties and collected tips from the men, but more importantly, she could build her own private cliental list.

Scarlet had found a new life. She rented a decent two-bedroom apartment and got a new car. Her apartment was large enough to accommodate private clients. Most of them from the upper middle class who just wanted to get away from the stress of everyday life. They wanted young girls who wanted sex their way, not the way their wives or girlfriends wanted. They wanted blowjobs or anal whenever they wanted. They did not want to deal with, "honey I have a headache," or, "I'm on my period," or, "not tonight honey," or the worst, "I've got PMS." Many men just wanted to pay for hot sex with young chicks they could simply change at will. It was also clear to Scarlet that many of the girlfriends and wives preferred their men would discretely see a prostitute than to bother them with their "perverse" needs. The word "discretely" was a key word in this case.

As a psychology student, she knew sex was not only stress relieving, but also a necessary activity for men's health—for his cardiovascular, immunological, and prostate functions in particular. She sometimes felt like savior to the men who entrusted themselves into her care. She played different roles for each client. First, of course, she would learn about his particular fantasies. She would find out what his "Trick" was since the "Trick" for one man was never the same for another. This was called a "Masturbatory Fantasy" in her textbooks.

Scarlet had another trick she called "Better than actual sex," or how to satisfy men sexually without having actual intercourse with them. This happened when striptease and particular fetish would give him such a kick that the intercourse became secondary. Clients could even finish the act themselves, usually.

Many clients had an innate desire to be treated like a child. A working girl then could play a role of a loving mother. The textbook name for it was "Infantilizing a man." It allowed the man to relax and enjoy the sex play while Scarlet took control.

This was the "Know how" that Scarlet was mastering through experience.

The womanly warmth of Scarlet, and sometimes even her motherly approach, was bearing fruit. Her number of steady clients was increasing.

Scarlet was not into S&M. It is not that she would be against the idea as such, but it just was not her cup of tea. She, however, practiced almost every other sexual variation and cherished them as an expression of human creativity.

Toni was a good "protector" for her and she paid him for security and for new client referrals.

Her schedule soon became so busy that she considered hiring a girl to work in the smaller bedroom, charging her half of the earnings for the room and referrals.

* * *

Life was good and the business was booming, but one should never believe good times will last forever.

Toni got in trouble. He was busted for running a prostitution ring and drug dealing. Scarlet knew the second charge was bogus. Toni simply was not paying enough to the cops or elected officials. His girls were highly successful in the men's clubs, making a lot of money for Toni and taking business from competing agencies and services. As a result, somebody made one of the club members testify against Toni in the prostitution case. The drug charges were later dropped in a plea bargain agreement.

Still, Toni had to do time and his girls remained without protection. Their choice was to either work for Toni's competitors for less money, or leave town. That was an easy choice—they stayed in town for less money. Scarlet stayed too as she had just six months left to finish school. Toni's competitors, however, would not allow her to keep all the money from private clients. They wanted half. She had a solid number of steady customers and they wanted that money for themselves. In other words, she had to work for them in their escort service and/or in a striptease joint.

Scarlet agreed with their conditions since she still had to complete school. She finished school and left town. In addition, she had to pay all kinds of "debts"—to pay off the bosses to let her go.

In the end, she boarded a bus and hit the road to start a new life in a new place. The new place was New York City and her new name was Katie.

* * *

So here she was, an out-of-town girl from Virginia, new to New York and trying to find a place to stay and conduct her business.

So what is there for a lone girl to do? She would go to clubs, discos and bars to meet men, not only a client for a night but, more importantly, to make connections with the city's upper and under-worlds. Life is full of surprises and you never know where you are going to find your luck. Imagine where Sharon Stone would be today if not the crotch scene without panties, shot accidentally (as she claims) for the movie "Basic Instinct."

Katie was particularly good with the "fallen men," who just yesterday climbed high mountains but today, needed reassurance that they were still strong and potent with a woman.

There were plenty of that type of men in the city, but this was not the end of Katie's goals. She needed a place where she could stay as well as conduct her business. Her underworld connections, which she gained thanks to the references from her home state, were not enough for her kind of goals. She needed to meet a "clean" man, a man of money and establishment with no connection to her underworld—a partner who would invest in her business, but not bother with the specifics.

When she studied psychology in college, she was particularly eager to learn about male psychology. This she also accomplished during her "social practice exercises," as she used to call it. She was aware it would not be easy to start her own business in NYC, but she was too ambitious to be easily discouraged. Besides, she was highly aware that her kind of educational credentials and professional experience was a solid foundation to build upon.

Katie's search for a sponsor, for a wealthy man who could be her sugar daddy or maybe a silent partner, did not go well at first. Her "underworld" contacts were mostly hustlers, pimps, and paparazzi that promised "protection" for pay with her eventual business. She had nothing to protect yet, but the "protectors" saw potential in Katie's looks and intelligence. She went to bed with some of them—"There is no free lunch," she used to say. They began inviting her to different NYC parties where she could make important contacts and meet rich older men who were frequenting these parties. Now this was closer to what Katie was looking for, but finding a sponsor would be a matter of luck and skill.

Finally, the day arrived. Mr. Burk, or just Allen for some, came from some kind of old money family, or so it was mentioned. Rumor had it that he had lost half of his fortune gambling. His age and mental condition were a topic of debate but nobody really cared. He paid the bills and loved to party with girls. That is all that really mattered.

He would sit in the most visible place and would chat with party girls with a thoughtful expression. The girls would sway around him in their sexy dresses, slightly touching his face and letting him smell their scent. Allen loved this entire ambiance and would then sponsor more parties for rising artists and models. He would go to restaurants with them and order drinks for everyone.

Katie was the new girl in the crowd and she carefully observed that nobody was eager to take care of Mr. Burk at the end of the party.

He was not anyone's client in real terms since he could hardly perform in bed. Katie knew she would have to do something different, something new, if she wanted to get somewhere with him.

Her chance arrived late one night as the party ended and girls quickly left for other places. Mr. Burk was still sitting with his "thoughtful" glassy look. Usually he would follow the girls, but this time he was too drunk and girls were too quick for him. Katie stayed and took care of him. She chatted with him and called a cab to take him home.

Mr. Burk did not feel well so she stayed with him overnight. He was sick and vomited several times. He could barely walk to the kitchen to get a glass of water.

Allen was bedridden for a few days after the party. Katie visited him daily and stayed another night when he ran a high fever.

Mr. Burk recovered within the week and Katie knew she had found her sugar daddy. Would he sponsor the kind of business she had in mind however? What would she do about his drunkenness and the wild parties? Could she take care of all the business alone? Well, she knew plenty of young girls eager to break into the business. The "Protectors" could help with clients and security, but they would need to get their share too.

Katie persuaded Allen that the profit surly exceeds the investment and the deal was made.

Katie started to run the shop. Mr. Burk, now the Silent Partner, put-up the initial money for a rent controlled three bedroom apartment in NYC's Upper East Side, where he had connections with the building's management.

The "Protectors" supplied the clients. Clients were instructed to tell the doormen that they were going to a counselor. They were given business cards that read: "Katherine Johns, M.A.—Counseling and Stress Reduction."

The building doormen and the other staff were paid off and any incidents that arose were dealt with quietly.

Clients addressed Katie as Miss Katherine. She embodied the gracefulness of the idea of a psychosexual caregiver for lonely men—married or single alike. She created such a professional atmosphere to the enterprise that it was soon nicknamed Katie's Clinic.

She no longer had to go to the bars and discos to look for clients. Miss Katherine dressed as a businesswoman and drove an expensive car, parking it in a clean garage under her luxury building. She could easily get to her apartment straight from the garage by elevator.

She was strict with the girls, but knew her place too. She was a chief counselor and supervised other girls' work. She herself had sex with selected clients only. Katie soon gained a respect of her staff and love of the clients as she listened and tried to understand them. She began implementing "Role Playing", where a girl would play the role of a client's wife, lover, secretary, or whoever satisfied his fantasy of sexual excitement. Complaints were few, clients were happy and the girls were afloat. Katie lived in one of the bedrooms of the same apartment.

* * *

Successful life soon became demanding, however. Katie worked so hard she hardly saw daylight. Allen was becoming something of a nuisance. He seemed to forget that this was just a business, not his family.

"Home and family is something no money can buy"—Katie told him once, though regretted it right away as he dropped his face into his hands and cried. He cried like a child who was just been told that his mother was not really his mother.

It took a lot of petting, kissing, and soft sexy talk to calm him down. He finally composed himself, looked straight into Katie's eyes and said:

"But I have no other family, no other wife."—Then he cried again.

Katie hugged him tight, kissed, and wiped his tears as they came like a rainfall. She kept him at her place that night, cuddling him and petting his head. He was like a child to her—a difficult child.

Two working girls Katie employed came to her place as to a normal job and worked until midnight. Katie was against late night hours as a matter of principal. The late night clients came from night bars where they drank too much and could not find a girl for a one-night stand. These guys were just looking for trouble. They could go to other places open until 2am or later.

The girls had their own personal needs too. If any of them needed to cry, it was on Katie's shoulder. She became a kind of mother to the girls. She felt like she should give more time to their needs, but everyone had their special problem, including the clients. Katie would have preferred to have steady clients only, if not this little thing called attachment. Imagine the attachment of a client to a whore—no other attachment felt stronger, not in many marriages anyway. Clients would fall in love with the girls, become jealous of other clients and it was then difficult to get rid of them.

Avoiding emotional involvement with a steady client was not easy. Katie once had to fire a working girl and a client alike. Constant training and supervision were clearly necessary. Girls who were highly sexual had another problem. They had a hard time suppressing their orgasm during sex. They climaxed too frequently and became exhausted. Finally, Katie took it on herself to teach girls how to suppress the orgasm during sex with clients. Katie also taught them to avoid full mouth French kisses. All this was necessary primarily to avoid emotional excitement and possible personal attachment to the client. The girls had to detach themselves emotionally from their clients; they had to fake it instead.

Some girls had no problem with it, however, since they could listen as therapists and satisfy clients' sexual fantasies. These were strong enough to get involved with steady clients, but avoid destructive emotional attachment. They were "born to be working girls", as Katie called them. Those were the girls with the "Gene of Prostitution"—according to Katie's own terminology. Katie knew that they could make good "high class prostitutes". Olga was one of them.

* * *

Ever since his meeting with Katie, Dr. J. started to have an obsessive desire to sneak into the apartment where Joshua had his sex-for-pay sessions. He suspected that Joshua was even having sex with Katie and wanted to catch them in the act. On the other hand, maybe it was just his voyeuristic wish to see Katie having sex with another man, other than himself. This kind of thought would come to his mind repeatedly.

Joshua felt better and was doing better, growing more self-confident day after day. He was becoming more assertive to his analyst, and everyone else in his life. Well, except his wife.

Dr. J. was beginning to wonder whether he wanted to experience what Joshua was going through. He, Jeffrey Glassman, M.D., psychiatrist, an Upper East Side Shrink, could not possibly desire to enter this whorehouse and have sex with prostitutes, could he? To be one of those men who pay for sex? To have sex with prostitutes who would let any man to have sex for-pay? The full picture was so disgusting and dirty to him that he had to willfully suppress those thoughts and think of ... soccer games of his children!

However, the suppression would only last a few hours. Those thoughts and images would return and he could not stop them. He was becoming sexually aroused. The dirtier the images, the more he felt the urge to masturbate. Finally, he had to start taking light sleeping pills to get a good night sleep.

He called Katie the next day after he met her in the elevator, to make an appointment to discuss Joshua's problems and ... to see her apartment. He realized the sooner he saw her place, the sooner he will get over his obsessive thoughts.

He felt very nervous when he entered Katie's apartment two days later, she looked fresh and relaxed, and there were fresh cut flowers on the living room coffee table. Katie was dressed in a short colorful sundress with a low neckline and, apparently, no bra.

He said he only had 30 minutes. "... and you want to talk about Joshua," she picked-up the sentence, "Why don't we go straight to my room in that case?"

Her room was the master bedroom with its separate bathroom. It had a small coffee table, and a desk with computer beside the large, well-decorated bed. They both set at the desk their knees almost touching. Dr. J. was suddenly aware of Katie's womanly scent and perfume. Her breasts were so close he could see her erect nipples. The odor combined with the view was mesmerizing. She looked stunning with smiling eyes and slightly open juicy lips. His heart skipped a beat when she touched his hand. They were suddenly kissing, kissing a deep open mouth kiss. No words were exchanged. He just could not keep his hands off her body, kissing her all over the face, all over her neck with the birthmark and her breasts with the hard nipples. Her dress seemed to come off by itself ...

God, her legs and buttocks were gorgeous, her underwear indescribable.

The next thing he knew they both were under the bedspread and it seemed like they were going to have intercourse. His heart was pounding as he tried to catch his breath.

Suddenly ... oh no! Not now! He almost jumped. There was a problem! He had just lost his erection! Katie was breathing heavily and felt wet. Dr. J. was speechless and shocked.

"Let me hug you, Jeff." She said, as she composed herself. "We really don't have to rush into the things. Come, snuggle with me." She hugged him tight and patted his hair.

"Sorry, this is the first time it happened to me. I haven't slept well last a few nights." He was apologizing.

Katie took his face into her hands and started to kiss him gently, his lips, eyes, nose, ears, and neck. Then she looked deep into his eyes.

"Hi, my name is Katie" — said she smiling.

"My name is Jeffrey ...

"May we kiss now, Jeff?" — She smiled, charmingly.

"I don't even remember when anybody called me Jeff, since my childhood."

They kissed and decided not rush into the sex—something what should really grow naturally. Dr. J. finished his coffee and it was time to leave. She hugged him at the door and said she would love to see him again.

* * *

That night Dr. J. took two sleeping pills and slept well. The next night he took only one pill, and slept well again. The next day he was seeing Katie. The thought of seeing his own analyst and discussing his encounter did come to his mind, but it was only a momentary thought. He took two hours from his schedule to visit her at the end of the day. There was no one else in the flat. Katie was dressed in a business suit. For the first hour, they hugged, kissed, and ate a little. Chatted a lot, smiled, and laughed. He had to control his hands, as he could not keep them from touching her. Katie reminded him to behave himself, as she sat him at the kitchen table and opened his favorite wine. Dr. J. was talking about a psychiatric conference where he was the keynote speaker, a very successful speaker. Katie listened, eating him with her eyes.

"Will you finally kiss your little girl?"—She asked as she sat on his lap smiling and looking into his eyes.

Jeff was excellent in bed that day. He was like a 20-year-old boy who just met the right girl. Katie could not stop admiring him. She kissed him a long, wet goodbye as Dr. J. left for the building garage to pick up his car and travel to his Westchester house. His exression was full of self-confidence and the pride of a sexually strong man. That night he slept without a sleeping pill for the first time in weeks.

He did not know that Katie gave him Viagra mixed in the food just an hour before the wonderful sex session they had.

What they do not know cannot hurt them—a lesson that Toni had once taught her.

* * *

It was back to business around the Katie's Clinic. Joshua was visiting his analyst 3 times a week and Olga once a week. He took a weeklong vacation with his wife, flying down to Paradise Island in the Bahamas, and came back refreshed. Allen looked like achieving some control in his drinking and was not complaining as often as before.

Dr. J. had scheduled meetings with Katie, but he called them dates and so did Katie. After the fiasco on their first date, Dr. J. had no more need for Viagra with Katie. He, however, did use it with his wife.

He thought about divorcing his wife at one point, as he became more comfortable with Katie. Katie quickly dissipated his thoughts, though. She asked him whether he intended to marry her, an American prostitute, or if he preferred Olga, a Russian prostitute. She pointed out to him how the society and his professional community would react to a successful Westchester psychiatrist wrecking his 15-year marriage and breaking up his family with two children. Katie could not have that on her conscience.

"But I love you Katie. Doesn't this mean anything? Doesn't this count for something?" He said it like only a teenager-in-love could say it.

"I love you too, Jeff. Do not ever doubt that."—She responded—"But remember, we are just the puppets of our society and must comply with its rules."—Katie hugged him and rested her head on his chest.

Dr. J. said he missed Katie in his life, but she promised to go on "vacations" with him, joining him while he was away at his conferences.

III

The vacations during the conference worked perfectly. Rebecca was never a jealous-type to check how many days the conference lasted, so Dr. J. was cutting short conference stay traveling instead with Katie.

"There is something else we can do together" — said Katie, once during their "vacation". He could become a psychiatric supervisor at Katie's Clinic. This would allow Katie's clients to call her services sex therapy and pay for it with their health insurance.

Dr. J. would have to sign health insurance claim forms, as the medical director. Katie's Clinic would have to be registered with various NY state authorities including the state police.

This was a talk they had after a wonderful night of lovemaking. He was enthusiastic at first—he did not see anything illegal in it. Surrogate sex therapy took off years ago in New York City. It was frowned upon by state agencies, but has never been prohibited.

He was personally familiar with one of the surrogate sex therapy clinics in the city and had even met the director and some staff members. It would be enough to get some of those members to train Katie's girls and things could be moving soon.

She thought the matter would be more complicated but agreed to talk about it on another occasion.

That occasion arrived during a psychiatric conference in Florida. Katie arrived three days before the conference ended.

Sex with Katie during the conference was great. Katie was good at putting new spice into a familiar meal. They sneaked at night into the main conference hall and made love on the same conference desk where he had chaired the session the day before.

Dr. J. was more amenable to accept Katie's ideas after these stormier "sessions." The idea of a legally run sex therapy clinic with surrogate sex partners as therapists, could not settle in Katie's mind however.

"Tell me more how surrogates would work in practice," asked Katie at the dinner. She was wearing a skimpy sundress scattered with spring flowers. Her cleavage was so deep he could almost see her nipples. Dr. J. could not find signs of any underwear on her body. Was she wearing anything underneath at all ...? He bought a gift for her day before—panties with garter belt and nylons—a French design.

"Surrogate girls are just a substitute for a real life girlfriend or wife," he answered while still eating dessert.

"And how are they different from real life prostitutes? They are substitutes too. Aren't they?"

"No, it's different. Surrogate girls know the psychological aspects of sexuality. Often they are unemployed psychologists or psychology students."

"Or any kind of gifted student girl with necessary assets who is attentive to the clients."—responded Katie.

"No, they have to be trained for that"—insisted Dr. J.

"Training is fine, that can be done, but how does it work in daily practice?"

Katie knew he loved to lecture.

"Suppose a guy goes to a family doctor and complains about a sexual problem—weak erection, premature ejaculation and so on. The doctor examines him and recommends a surrogate sex therapy clinic. We know that most of the sexual problems are purely psychological. Once in that clinic he has a forty-five minute talk with a therapist and then a forty-five minute session with a trained surrogate. That trained young, sexy girl works both psychologically and physically through his insecurity. Starts with little erotic touches and then proceeds with partial penetration. The condom is a must, of course."

"Let me guess—there would be no kisses, no deep eye to eye looks, or any sexy smiles"—Katie commented—"and of course no sexy skirts and panty-flashing allowed."

"That is right. In addition, the clinic and everyone working there must be registered with state licensing agencies. The clinical director must be a licensed M.D. He would also be the official business owner and responsible for paying malpractice insurance and taxes."

"Ok. I agree, let's do it."—She said with a playful smile,—"You go, and get registered as a clinical director and business owner of the Sex clinic."

Dr. J. paused.

"You know, truth is that the whole thing is being looked at as an immoral enterprise by other official medical and psychiatric establishments."—He spoke slow, measuring and weighting every word—"It may not be a good idea for me with my academic career ..."

"To get involved with a sex clinic because they are viewed as whorehouses?" —Ended his thought Katie—"It's the sex for money no matter what you call it. Isn't it so Jeff?" —Katie nailed it, so to speak. Dr. J. fell silent for a while.

"Moreover, sex clinics have to register with the police department too,"—she continued—"and my girls would then be registered in the police computers as 'taxpaying prostitutes'."

"That's what the law requires"—he finally spoke and knew that the registered sex clinic was not a good idea. They sat a while in silence.

"So the easiest way would be me just billing your clients for psychotherapy sessions—the sex sessions which you would provide."—He paused again.

"But you can meet them and talk to them. They will all benefit from it"—spoke in low voice Katie— "It, however, should be your decision, Jeff."

"Clients will have to sign, that they did receive therapy." Dr. J. was now in a somber mood and he was becoming pale as he spoke. He could almost hear his own heartbeat.

"But that's criminal, outright criminal!" His voice became firmer.

"Jeff, but you know that men need sex to stay fit."

"What about masturbation? Doesn't it help?"

"Yes, it helps, but cannot substitute the sex itself. This of course supports the prostitution." Partners become like one person during the sexual intercourse. They enter each other in more ways than just anatomically. Partners' simultaneous orgasm is something irreplaceable for their health and happiness. This kind of simultaneous orgasm is only achieved with full genital contact—without a condom.

"It sounds like the natural sexual contact works as a 'Happiness Hormone'."

"After all, it's like going to GYM to stay fit..."

"Tell me, do health insurance companies pay for preventive care, I mean a prevention of disabilities?"—asked she with a particular look as if suddenly something came to her mind.

"Yes, insurance pays when there is a well-proven efficacy."

"What about prevention of prostate cancer? Is this good enough reason for Health Insurance to pay for its prevention?"

"... I am ... not sure about it."

"But you just said that regular sex is irreplaceable for men's health."

"Yes, this is true."—said he unwillingly, as if he did not want to admit it.

"So, why can't we just open a clinic for prevention of prostate diseases? Don't people take eye glasses when they get older?"

"Well, medical care of the future is supposed to be Preventive care. In case there is a decrease of prostate cancer, the state would also save health expenses."

"Yes Jeff that would save tax payers' money." Katie was clearly excited as Jeffrey was just finishing her thoughts.

"Practically it would mean that I would bill health insurance companies for clients having sex with you." He suddenly felt little stunned of what he just said. He was silent for a minute and then added, "So ... why not? It's actually logical ... it would be for the benefit of the client, the state, and the public. Clients would be happier, the public healthier, and the state would save tax money."

"This is an excellent idea sweetheart—we will bill insurance companies only for men in their middle-advanced age. Young ones will pay from their own pocket." Katie was facing Jeffrey looking deeply into his eyes. She took his hand and said in a soft voice—"Jeffrey, my sweetheart, don't do anything you don't feel comfortable with." She hugged him—"You are an honest doctor, a knight on a white horse, but you know most of the doctors cheat on insurance companies. Think about the therapy following car accidents. They are all grossly exaggerated. You do know it."

Dr. J. was quietly looking somewhere far. She approached and patted his graying hair.

"Everybody is getting paid by the insurance from the medical business, even their lawyers, and the ambulance drivers."—Katie was kissing and patting him like as if he was a little child.

"I know"—he said looking tired—"the insurance companies make money too. It gives them reason to raise premiums."

"Or that psychiatrist, old friend of yours, who proclaimed himself a financial advisor for retired people in Florida; teaching them psychological schemes how to make money on stocks. He knows it is all bullshit but charges them $1000 to attend his one day seminar."

"Yah, moreover, he is a psychoanalyst too. He totally lost shame"—said sadly Jeffrey.

Katie looked into his eyes like a kitten wanting him to take care of. He was aware that their exciting love affair has been getting costly. He could no longer withdraw from his family savings as his wife was becoming suspicious. Dr. J. needed an extra source of income that his wife would not know about.

The next thing he knew he was engulfed by Katie's scent. He felt as if he was drowning... smelling her perfume mixed with the familiar body aroma. He was suddenly in the bed when he opened his eyes. Both were still partially dressed; she had her heels and skirt on. Katie was kissing him all over while lying on top of him. He grabbed her sexy bottom and pulled her to his face so she could straddle his head and he could smell her familiar aroma— the aroma of the most desirable Rosebud in the universe. Her skirt was the one he bought for her, but the panties... (He did not buy these orange panties and he never saw them on her before... so who... who bought them?) He moved the fabric of her orange panties aside and almost fainted from her intoxicating sexy smell. The euphoric pleasure was too much to stand and he lost self-control. He felt humiliated being so powerless ...but it was too late for these thoughts. He was kissing her Rosebud passionately with a full mouth kiss, as if kissing a woman's real lips. The scent and taste so powerful that were easily capable of enslaving a man in the sweetest bondage.

He was floating out of his body hearing the songs of mystic Sirens from out of space...

Dr. J. was done and the deal was forged!

* * *

Life at Katie's Clinic moved to another level— it started to bloom. Dr. J. insisted on seeing every client for whom he signed insurance forms. This became complicated as clients came to see the girls and not the shrink. Soon there were so many claim forms to process they had to hire a billing person to take care of them. Eventually business was running smoothly and money started to flow. Katie expanded working hours, hiring more girls. She became so busy that Dr. J. began to complain she did not have time for him. Katie would respond telling him to devote more time to his wife and children.

Dr. J. no longer had to pay for trips or dinners with Katie; she paid them as business expenses. There was enough money for all. He wanted to see all aspects of Katie's life, but that did not work out as she cherished her privacy. He was getting suspicious, but felt ashamed to say anything too loud.

In the end, he suffered quietly. He was increasingly jealous of her and suspected her of being unfaithful. The feeling both tormented and excited him at the same time. The whole thing was becoming painful and clearly masochistic, so he finally decided to put an end to his suspicions. He decided to drop by unexpectedly and check what was going on in her private room when he was not there.

One day he finally found the proof of his suspicions. He quietly entered Katie's place with his key, and went to her personal room, sneaking into the closet. He waited not knowing exactly how long it will take. The fact that he, a respected professor and psychoanalyst was hiding in a prostitute's closet to spy on her, gave him a strange rush of excitement. The rush became a buzz with a pounding heartbeat once she finally entered the room with a stranger.

He was well dressed, tall, masculine… and black… African-American—correctly speaking! It looked like they were having a business meeting. Katie was in a short white skirt with black stockings seamed in the back. She was also wearing high heels and sheer blouse. They sipped coffee and discussed some documents, which the gentleman took out of his briefcase. Katie crossed her legs and tried to prove her points simply, trying to deal to her advantage. Then she stood up, walked around, and sat next to the man moving close to his face with her low cut cleavage. Dr. J. could literally smell her bodily odor as it engulfed the man. The stranger could not stand it for long. He made an agreeable gesture to her suggestions and put his hand on her bottom. Katie looked straight into his dark eyes.

"No, it's not that simple. You need to sign a document first. Over here, please."—she pointed to the spot with her angelic finger. The gentleman signed the paper in silence and looked into her eyes as he moved his hand under her skirt.

"No, this wasn't part of the deal,"—she smiled a glowing smile, the smile of a winner,—"Your signature is good, but there are more papers to sign and more deals to make, so tomorrow, perhaps." She moved his hand from her thigh and patted his arm delicately.

Suddenly all hell broke loose. The gentleman reared up like a "predator", growled, and grouped her bottom moving his hand back under her skirt. He hugged her forcefully and started to kiss her on the mouth. Katie struggled a moment, but then opened her mouth for a real French kiss. The man's hand moved wildly under her skirt and her white panties flashed. Katie became quite restless.

"No, no... not now, and not here! This is enough for today."

The man looked like he was in a shock. —"Give me the rest of the damn papers. I'll sign them now!"

Katie slowly opened a drawer and took out five documents.

"Sign them lover, right here, in this spot!" —The gentleman signed. She then touched his groin and gave a sexy look. Dr. J. felt like jumping out of his skin since his own erection was now painfully pressing against the fabric. Katie kissed the Afro-American with a wet kiss, turned her bottom to the man, and bent over to clean the signed papers off the desk.

Her bending over was evidently too much for him. He groped her, raised her skirt over her round bottom, and the doctor saw her lace laden white panties... These were the panties Dr. J. had gifted her a day before.

Dr. J. was devastated, but his sexual arousal became uncontrollable at this point and the strongest ever orgasm overwhelmed him. Katie screamed with her own pleasure as the "predator" started to grunt with a kind of growl that Dr. J. has never before heard. Dr. J. bit his tongue not to scream, then leaned on the clothes inside closet and fainted.

Dr. J. regained his senses only when Katie opened the closet door. She jumped in shock. The "predator" was gone. Dr. J. now saw closely her sexy legs. She had opened the closet to find a towel to clean herself up.

"Oh Jeff...! You are here, my poor sweetheart?" She tried to help him to his feet, but instead he crawled under her skirt and kissed her messy thighs. Katie touched his cheek and removed his eyeglasses.

"I know what you need baby... come here, come to mama." —She slowly raised her skirt and lowered herself onto his mouth. He drove Katie to another orgasm, as they made love right there, in the closet.

Katie passed him her used, already torn white panties, once it was over.

"Take these as a gift from my heart. These panties will surely give you an extra kick any time..." —He looked at Katie with the eyes of a child who had just done something very mischievous and was begging his mom for forgiveness. She smiled and warmly hugged him.

That was it. Dr. J's life changed from that day. He stopped worrying about little things, as his wife's complains about not enough money, or about Katie being unfaithful to him, or even about him signing fraudulent health insurance claims for the whorehouse clients.

He would usually hide in Katie's room, waiting for her to return with a client. Then he would watch them having sex from the closet. Sometimes they would have a threesome together. His psychiatric practice and university teaching did not suffer as much as one might expect, though Dr. J. did have a hard time to concentrate.

Katie later helped him to become more comfortable with his newly found sexual lifestyle. Strangely, it made him feel more self-confident. There was almost a feeling of rebellion against an oppressive society with its unwritten rules. As if, he did not want to be a puppet any longer. Yes, he now felt liberated through his secret war against the medical, psychiatric, and other official establishments. All of them who put him in his golden cage—the psychoanalytic office—to receive the confessions of poor souls and turn them into *politically correct* conformists and workaholics. Not into liberated and Libertine men or women they could be.

Everyone in this society should conform to the unwritten rules of social acceptability. All should be puppets of society and find happiness within its limited freedom. That was what he, professor Jeffrey Glassman, M.D. was supposed to preach to his students at the University; so that, there would be more psychiatrists to convert more people into *correct* citizens.

Dr. J. was supposed to breed happy conformist "doctor—puppets". The doctors who would work hard to pay their Taxes, Insurances, Double Mortgages, Leases, Loans, Babysitters, School Payments, Tutors, Nurses, Caretakers, Housekeepers, House-sitters, Maintenance Bills, Therapy Bills, Lawyers' Bills, Medical Bills, Alimonies, Donations, and even bills for their own eventual funeral. ... And finally would die soon after they retired, if they ever retired. There was no other life for them than hard work, not in this world. They might as well realize that they have only been "Cash Cows" enriching banks, middlemen, and all kinds of extras around.

Dr. J. was sitting mesmerized with his thoughts—all of these, though so easy to comprehend, never occurred to his mind before. He was never a free man and never will be; he just went in circles his whole life. "Life is hard and then you die"—the old American saying felt as custom made for him. Jeffrey was glad that finally could open his eyes on the reality and see it as just it was. Nonetheless, doubts were lingering in his mind—his newly discovered libertine philosophy would be difficult to apply to real life out there.

His relationship with his wife was as formal as ever. Before, she was the one who was "just doing her spousal duty in the bed". Now there were two of them "doing the duties". She did not notice any change in husband's behavior, as she was not interested in his intimate life. This clearly showed to Jeffrey that she had never truly loved him and he, probably, never loved her either. The only one who had ever loved him was Katie with her libertine lifestyle ... and he was addicted to her.

He never contacted his old psychoanalyst and certainly did not talk to any of his colleagues about his new "Psychosexual Level of Functioning".

* * *

Dr. J. opened his office with those thoughts, and signed number of insurance forms for the prostitutes' clients to be sent to health insurance companies. He was still preoccupied with the thoughts of his new Libertine Philosophy and had difficulty to concentrate at work. Meanwhile his first patient was already talking about his own problems, which he was supposed to deal with. He was finally able to get rid of disturbing thoughts and to focus on the patient's story.

Joshua was going through similar marital problems like Dr. J. His wife was not responding to his efforts of sexual awakening. She just made love for Joshua once a week as a spousal duty. His relationship with Olga, his sex therapist and surrogate sex partner, was another thing. He could not help comparing Olga with his wife. Regardless of all the moral, social, and financial advantages, his wife was losing in the comparison. There was something plain and honest about Olga—she was a prostitute who was sexually involved with him for all 60 minutes. She was as honest as Dr. J., who was fully psychologically involved with Joshua for 45 minutes. He was also visiting a rabbi in his town synagogue to keep his relationship with God clean. However, since none of them could predict the future, Joshua took a colleague's advice and contacted a Psychic as well. Now he really felt that he was safe. He spent virtually all his free time going to those advisors—from the rabbi and psychiatrist to the psychic and prostitute. Dr. J. told him once—

"It must feel like walking with four crutches through life."

"I was still little when parents took me to talk to a rabbi. That was my first crutch."—Then paused and added,—"But you doctor are the biggest all of those crutches—officially recognized and *Politically Correct*, one who is even paid partly by health insurance; someone I can proudly put onto my CV. Olga the prostitute, however, is my shameful secret crutch,"—said Joshua starring at Dr. J's diplomas on the wall,—"and she is the one who perhaps helps me most."

It came to Dr. J's mind at this point, that Joshua probably was more sane and assertive than he himself. He could actually stop psychotherapy at this point. This thought, though, did not last long—Joshua also was a three times a week, well-paying patient, and his termination would not do any good to the doctor's family budget. Besides, the patient definitely has a problem in his family life. Therefore, he had better continue treatment.

Joshua's wife, of course, did not even know about Olga's or the psychic's existence. She did not know he was having sex with a prostitute next door from the therapy office, and this cheating was going on with his psychiatrist's consent—the psychiatrist who was paid from her family's money. The payments for Olga, the rabbi and psychic came out from Joshua's earnings as a stockbroker. He claimed at home that he had a bad luck and was losing on the stock market.

They did not have kids and that was a blessing—at least that is how Joshua felt by now. His work was going fine and he was content with his life while meeting Olga regularly. She actually helped him more than Dr. J's psychoanalysis. He wanted to see Olga more often than he saw Dr. J., and that was a problem—she was becoming his soul-mate as well.

There was Dr. J. and the rabbi, playing the role of Joshua's tolerant father and Joshua's wife as the controlling Jewish mother. Olga was a lover, and the psychic—his secret advisor. One could say it was like a typical New York family, so to say.

Joshua himself just felt like shutting everybody out and jumping into Olga's bed, like a little boy.

IV

This "program" of Stress Reduction and Psycho-analysis functioned for another three years in the Upper East Side. However, as they say in New York *whatever goes up must come down* one day.

Katie's clinic was in existence until Allen Burk was alive. Unfortunately, the Gods did not give him a long time. After his death, his rent-controlled apartment, where Katie's Clinic was located, had to be vacated. Katie and Olga, however, would not move out and hoped that Dr. J. could make a deal with the landlord. However, they could not stay since they were not Mr. Burk's family members and their name was not on the lease. Moreover, the landlord has recently made capital improvements to the building, which gave him the right to terminate the rent-controlled leases as the tenant died.

Dr. J's involvement made things even worse. His office has been in a rent-controlled apartment as well and the lease allowed only residential use. He appealed to management on behalf of Katie's Clinic to allow "Psychological services" in the late Mr. Burk's apartment. Then he inadvertently told them he himself had a psychiatric office next door, he learned the bitter truth. They would *all* have to leave. The rent controlled apartment lease clearly stated that the premises were for residential purposes only. This way he also revealed his association with Katie and her prostitutes. It came out that the doormen had been regularly reporting all the activities of the Clinic to the management. They knew everything but no one had said anything up to this point out of respect for Allen Burk. Unfortunately, Dr. J. did not have the connections, late Mr. Burk used to.

One nice sunny day a sudden hailstorm came down from high above. Dr. J., the psychoanalyst and university professor, got caught with his pants down, literally. He was at Katie's clinic "supervising her clinical work"— having sex with Katie and Olga while dressed in ladies underwear. A private detective, hired by the management, entered the premises quietly and began filming everything with his mobile phone. The doormen and building superintendent accompanied him as witnesses.

Suddenly all hell broke out. Dr. J. and the girls, all felt as if they were in a horror movie. Later, the story even made it to TV Channel 1 "News for New York" and Dr. J's photographs with Katie appeared on "Page Six" of the New York Post.

The list of criminal charges was long including even Mail and Computer Fraud. However, the most prominent were fraudulent medical billing, and running an upscale prostitution ring from an Upper East Side luxury condo; the building where he also practiced Psychiatry and Psychoanalysis.

Technically speaking, he was charged with being a pimp and using his Medical License to steal money from insurance companies. "Fraudulent billing is a felony, which Criminal Code calls simply Grand Larceny"—explained the prosecutor. His wife Rebecca told the media that they had been all, but separated for some time and refused to see him from the moment the story broke up. She quickly divorced him and received most of joint assets in the settlement. She then moved with the children to her parents' house and later bought a house on her own on Long Island.

Katie took a deal which the prosecutor offered, and testified against Dr. J.; this was his own wish as well. He told her while in jail before the trial— "I am a dead-man anyway; your testimony could not possibly make it worse. I want you to live and prosper as a psychologist—you do have a talent for it. You have become like a daughter to me for last three years." Katie hugged him and he spoke more. "My love, you need a career and a real, normal life: meaning whatever society considers normal and politically correct. You see, you were right Katie. We are all puppets of our social-political culture, after all." He paused and then added, "And so shall we remain in order not to be social outcasts". Then he hugged Katie tight, and buried his face on her breast; hugged her as only babies hug their mother's breast. Well, whatever happens in jail should remain inside the jail.

New York State Supreme Court convicted Jeffrey Glassman, M.D. for two years. He did not appeal the sentence as his lawyer advised him. He saw no point in it. Jeffrey was also running empty in his bank account and lawyers do not work free.

The New York State Medical Board revoked his license and the insurance companies, which he had defrauded, obtained a large financial judgment against him (including interest and penalties). His savings were not enough to pay even the legal fees, however. At the end, the bankruptcy court placed a lean on everything he still owned; including his lawyers' lean on his possible future income. They made sure to receive their legal fees, though defending him with no apparent success. He was soon transferred to an upstate correctional facility to serve the sentence.

Katie and Olga walked free in exchange for cooperating with the prosecution. Katie went back to Virginia Beach and moved back with Toni who was just released from prison; before the term for good behavior.

The end of Joshua's story with Olga and his wife was truly sweet. He could no longer stand his wife's fake orgasms and once started to strangle her during the act. He, however, quickly came to his senses and left her alone shouting: "Why can't you just say that you don't feel anything ... or just lay there till I'm finished!" These were his *famous last words* before breaking an expensive crystal chandelier, a wedding gift, and running out of the house.

A rumor has it that Joshua took half of family's savings and decided to leave this Technocratic world.

Probably he was fed up with being controlled by others, self-controlled, and having to control others. He flew with Olga to Russia, far into Siberia, where no gimmicks of western civilization could catch them.

They lived there for some time, but Olga hated the Siberian winters and decided this was not a place for her. She was already too Americanized. Joshua on the other hand loved the wild nature and not having to go to work to Wall Street. Subsequently, Olga moved back to Big Apple and back to the harsh, but glamorous world of the oldest profession.

Joshua settled in the Siberian Jewish town of Birobidzhan and claimed to be an American rabbi. He told everyone that he moved to this Siberian community because of his religious beliefs.

Two years passed (time passes slowly in Siberia) and Joshua received a letter from Olga in New York. It came out that his wife divorced him in absentia—for the Reason of Abandonment since Joshua was missing for more than one year. She was also planning to re-marry—she probably found a guy who liked her the way she was. She never filed any charges against Joshua—not even for alimonies. Therefore, Joshua did not have to pay any divorce settlement and could come back to New York. He was already homesick for the Big Apple by that time.

Joshua returned to NYC wanting to marry Olga, but there was a problem—Joshua's family insisted on Olga's conversion to Judaism. She claimed, on the other hand, that she was an atheist, and would not make a mockery of Joshua's religion. She refused to convert to Judaism regardless of Joshua's promise she could continue working in an escort service even after their marriage. Olga, on the other side, would rather give up prostitution than to recognize any kind of God.

Now—try to figure out, who is normal and who is mad.

KGB Agent: Mr. Hemingway—
Et Tu Brute, Erneste? *

Rhymed Essay

The world had just gone
  out of its fricken mind.
Who was the KGB spy?—
  Ernest Hemingway?
He had enlisted
  on his own free will,
    under the code-name "Argo"—
    so it is written on a sheet
    at the KGB archives
      in Moscow.
Was it really worth it, Ernesto?
Did your social liberalism get you?
Or did they get you for something
  so intimately secret to you?
What was that, how did they get you?
  what went through your
    genial mind?
      Why did you do it?

---

* The source: "Spies: The Rise and fall of the KGB in America", by John E. Haynes.
  Yale University Press, 2009

Perhaps—
They got you during the Spanish Civil War,
    when you, with your Parisian liberal brains,
Refused to see the real reality,
    that the Spanish people were
        behind General Franco,
not with the International intellectuals,
    like you.
So you twisted the truth and wound up
    on the same side of the barricades as the Commies,
        as Josef Stalin and his bloody
            Soviet-Russian troops—
So called "International" fighters,
    fighting Spaniards and Franco.
Just to mention, that you, as a war journalist,
    never even mentioned
        the presence of the Soviet troops in Spain.
You did not mention it
    in your novel either—
"To Whom the Bell Tolls",
    to note
But you mentioned there
    a Moscow reporter,
who was all powerful,
    with "High level" ties.
Whom you did befriend and preferred
    over the other reporters—
        your Western friends.
Was it that man who twisted your arm?

Was it then when you misread
   the very nature of the war and
      misled your readers
         about the Spanish Civil War?
It was there that you signed up with the Commies,
   I mean—the Soviet Russian Commies?
      There you became a KGB spy!?—
How do we know that?—
   Russians now
      revealed it themselves.
And they say
   you were the real enthusiast,
      willing to help by all means.
Just that they didn't find
   much of a use for you.
Later, though, you really helped them
   when you sided with the bandit Castro
      and his Cuban Commie revolution.
You even met him publicly,
   and the photos went around
      the entire world.
What a propaganda blitz!
And all the leftist intellectuals
   followed you as a beacon.
What a treat it was for the KGB.
   Surely the old friend of yours—
      the Moscow reporter,
         was honored and promoted
            for recruiting you
               for the KGB.

The horror of the matter is,
  my former idol Ernesto,
    that you are not alone
    in your demise.
There were some others like you too—
Milan Kundera, from the latest—
  the icon of the European scene.
And many others, the leftist-minded,
  all anti-American.
But you are so far
  the biggest American name
    on that list.
Just to imagine, on the other side,
  that so many plain Russians
  and Eastern Europeans,
Free-standing poets and writers,
  were jailed in Gulag, Siberia,
    but never gave up,
      never signed up with the KGB.
Just to mention one—Joseph Brodsky,
Later honored as a Russian-American poet,
  the Nobel winner, like you.
He was jailed in Russia,
  during his youth, for "vagrancy"
    while he wrote his "anti-Soviet" poetry.
Year and a half of hard labor—
just for trying to be a free poet!
Another name?—Pasternak,
  author of "Doctor Zhivago".

Not to mention Solzhenitsyn,
     author of "The GULAG Archipel-
ago",
     and so many others.
Why they were jailed?—Because
     they never sided with evil.
Just one nod to KGB
and they could have been freed,
     and made into official,
          prosperous Soviet writers.
But they refused!
And You, ... Why *you* ...?
Et tue Brute—Ernesto?
Thanks God that Charles Bukowski
     is no longer alive
          to learn that horrific fact
               of your KGB demise.
Bukowski, who once honored you
     with the words
"... But to me, the twenties centered
     mostly on Hemingway,
Coming out of the war
     and beginning to type."
Charlie, now flying in his heavens,
     above us all,
Would probably say:
     "I can't believe it, Ernie!
But if it's true, you must be down,
     in a dark hell now"

And he would later say some more:
"Ernie, you son-of-a-bitch,
  You've disgraced us all.
May all the Gods now cast
  the final judgment on you!"
Who knows, after all
  why you shot yourself.
Maybe to restore your name?
  Maybe your pride finally woke up?
Or perhaps, you woke up yourself
  once you witnessed
    Castro's bloody enslavement
    of his own people.
The Soviet kind of enslavement—
  the KGB style.
You took a shotgun into your hands,
  in the wee hours of the morning, and ...
Like a bleeding bull in the corrida,
  that knows he will be dead,
    still charges one last time
      to stand with pride
        till finally dead.
That's the bull's last Charge,
  like one from your shotgun.
The just suicide of a writer
  who served the wrong side
    and who lied to his readers.
The rightful and well-deserved,
  but still honorable
    suicide of yours.

Free Kisses

Rhymed Stories and Frivolous Poems

I
From Prague, Paris, Spain and Brazil

To Muse
To the One Whose Name Cannot Be Mentioned

Last night, it seems,
   I had been out of my mind.
I have written you ... a poem
   hope you don't mind
I found it in the morning,
   since I was drunk last night
It was in disarray, although it said
   all what I wanted to say.
I fixed it this morning,
   made it more plausible,
Linguistically palatable,
   and socially acceptable
Though it was more honest
   When I was drunk last night

So, here is your poem:

When there is nothing
   anymore to drink
When there isn't
   even food for thought
When there isn't
   anymore hope left
We are just left
   with love
    to dream about.

My distant Muse,
   this letter is to you
Not to as mortal human
   or as to an earthly girl,
    at all,
But as to someone,
   who as the princess of universe,
Is very busy with the princes
   adoring her charms
    of course.
My letter shall come
   as just another song
Song of another
   broken heart
Of another knight
   fallen for your charms.

And even though
   we can never be together
For the reasons
   well known to us
Allow me to at least
   keep you close to my heart
As a violet of the youth
   as a reminder of my past.

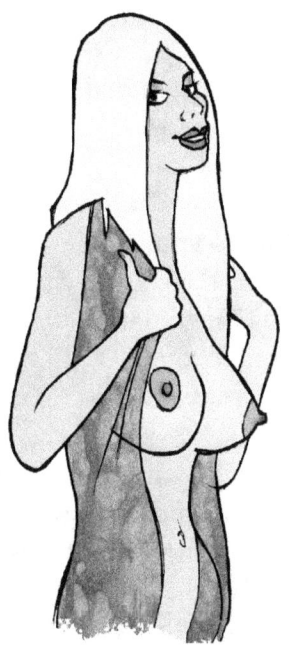

The Elegant Lily
Ballad of a Lost Innocence

My beautiful, elegant Lily
Oh, why did I meet you so early?
I was still young and innocent
And you—a star and a beauty!

Nightly streets crowded with people,
And then you ran into me,
  smelling like flowers,

So divine, elegant and airy
The scent of yours
  gave me weak knees.

You took me to your place
The room was dark and I was pale
I saw you as Magdalene
Couldn't touch you,
  unable to undress.

We chat a while, you spoke of your life,
Cracked a joke, and we shared some wine.
Then you drank more and spoke of hardships,
Tough childhood
  and many heartbreaks

Of lonely mother, father that failed,
The honor and pride that never paid
I held your hands, and you cried
You touched my heart,
  and I hugged you tight.

Suddenly, I touched your breast,
A sensation I never before felt
You pressed me with your thighs,
And I melted,
  dissolving into sighs.

"Oh Lily ... Lily, God ... so innocent ..."
My first night was short but passionate
I kissed your lips,
    discovering your ears
You cuddled with me—
    that was better than sex.

At daybreak, once night was done
I was still patting your hair with love.
Then someone knocked—
    we had to be gone.
You kissed me—"bye"
    and I knew—we wouldn't last.

I cried later, when I learned of your trade
I got attached—it was hard to break
You were my first,
    you couldn't be for sale
I wished you with me,
    to run and to sail.

I left the city, with you in my heart,
What could I offer to change your life
I was dead poor,
    you couldn't be my wife
So, I kept you as the elegant
    for the rest of the life.

My beautiful, elegant Lily
Oh, why did I meet you so early?
Each time, the night is done
    and the day breaks
I call you back:
    "Let me pat your hair
        with love, again".

Don't Leave Me Now
To Janina

Snow will melt and rain will fall
Days will go and darkness will come
The sun will set and again dawn,
But you will never,
     never come.

I dreamed last night of life and death
There was a demon, haunting me
Then something came and saved me
Was that your smile?
     so strange to me ...

Winter is white and roofs are red
Snow is real but it will melt
Flakes will fly and heart will beg
Don't leave me now,
    please don't melt.

Darkness will go and days will come
Spring will follow the winter
Snow will melt and rain will come
But you will never,
    never come.

In Paris—with the Drifter Girls

I found once some drifter girls
They slept embraced on the city stairs,
Maybe somebody could help the girls,
With the world asleep, nobody cared.

What is the real cost of love,
How much is that sex and trash
Where is the girl I used to love?
Is there a place where I can crash?

I am on Montmartre, under the stars
Music is crazy with loud drums and beats
The girls wake up; they giggle and dance
They kiss each other, smoking the grass.

Playing among stars and shameless girls
I couldn't resist—danced and swayed with them
Let the whole world sleep in their beds
I'll sleep on the stairs with the drifter girls.

Return to Montmartre—to the Home Gone

To Janina

I am on Montmartre where I once belonged,
Belonged as the cobblestones, as the trees.
Climbing the stairs we used to run
Looking for loose gold on the streets.

Passing the same streets and the empty stores
The dead art-dealer still behind his doors
Looking for refuge and close souls,
Since you left me and closed the doors.

Finding the house where you once lived
When we held our hands, played and dreamt,
But the last time, when we played the tricks
I got messed up, slipped, and killed our dream.

I completed the journey, I came back.
You are gone, but your spirit is still there
The dead art-dealer will welcome me back
But you—will you ever, ever come back?

Under the Montmartre Stars
With Wine and Sweetest Drifter Girls

To God-damn Charley ... Bukowski

It's Friday night in Paris,
  there is a full moon
    up in the sky
Thank God it's not the 13th
  or the world would
Surly go bananas
  out there in Paris
Or maybe
  the world is crazy anyway
but we don't yet know
  about it.

I went to Paris for a nice girl,
  but found an empty place there
She was there, but for me she wasn't -
  my habits did not agree with hers.
So I had to switch to a Montmartre bar
  settle in,
    and drink damn cheap wine there.
Met some drunks, tourist girls,
  and whores—my sisters.
The girl I came to Paris for
  went with some other guys.

She had no regrets
    and neither had I.
Then I dreamed
    with wine and stars
        on the Montmartre stairs
Got boozed, stoned, and even laid
    with some drifter girls.
Daybreak came with birds singing
    and the girls snoring.
Sunrise gets crazy there—
    on Montmartre.
Paris trip, though aimless,
    wasn't wasted after all,
Thanks to the cheap wine and,
    the sweetest drifter girls.

Girls dump you and then
        you dump them in return.

Lousy Rainy Night in Paris' Streets
To God-damn Charley ... Bukowski

It's a lousy
    rainy night
        in Paris' streets ...

I'm not even drunk yet,
but the barman already announces
    "Last Call".
They close too early here,
    I call this the Bar of Fast Drinks—

That is, to make me drink fast,
 pay fast,
  and get me out of here
   same fast.

There was a girl from Quebec,
 in the next bar,
  interested in my mumblings
She was smart and proper,
 and brainy too
But I needed
 something else,
  for tonight.

So I left her, and walked to rue St. Denis.
There was an American bar—
Front Page they'd named it,
 where I could keep boozing
  till 5 in the morning.
At the end,
 I didn't really have time
  for their girls—
 the homeless and drifters
 that served as hookers there.

Tonight though
 a Polish girl approached me
  to talk before the end.

She finally laid me …
  and got paid,
    before I passed
    in there.

The morning woke me
  to a big headache
    and the smell of paint.
I was on Montmartre,
  in a fake-art dealer's
    storage room,
Filled with fake art
  and fake booze.
He was an alien like me
  and had pity for me.

I crawled out to the rainy streets—
full of people,
    but empty for me.

Walked to a bar
    and asked for Demi.
They gave me beer,
    "Here, she'll no longer be."
So, I drank the beer as if I didn't mind.
Drank another one ...
    and then it came to my sick mind
That perhaps, I too,
    should finally fake something
        out of my life,
So I wouldn't look
    like crazy loser,
        I really was.

The only people
    I knew around
That didn't have to fake
    anything at all
Were the girls
    from rue St. Denis,
But even they had to fake it
    with their clients
        sometimes.

Dirty Dancer
In Prague "Popo-Club"

It was a Gipsy Night
  in the Popo club, in Prague
The Gaitanis played the music
  and a gipsy beauty
    swung and danced.
Her eyes were all in smile and
  her thighs seductively flashed,
    making the crowd to move and dance.

The night before, though, I saw her
    in another neighborhood.
There were no streetlights,
    just some shadows
        in the full moon.
She was drunk and vulgar,
    and was cursing too.
The other girls apparently,
    were all whores around her.
Their hips in short skirts, high heels and
    stockings, filled with desire
        and filthy pleasures.
Flashing their hips in the short skirts,
    with the stockings and heels,
Filled with desire
    and filthy pleasures
        offering their flesh for cash.
I walked up to the dancer
    and asked the price for her.
She said she was not
    for sale there.
That I could have any other
    but not her.
Some others were good too,
    but not as good as her
Then a stretch limo drove up
    and a fat guy came out of it.
The whores got startled
    and stared at him

The girl, the one not for sale,
　　walked up to the guy
　　　and kissed his hand.
The hand handed her some coins
　　and she bowed in return.
The others glanced with envy at her
She then followed him to the car
　　with slow steps
　　　swinging her hips as a slut
The fat guy even pinched her ass
　　entering the car with her.

The crowd got wild with the dancer
　　her legs flashing
　　　with the laughter.
The Gaitanis hit the music
　　her hands moving along her body
　　　brushing her thighs and the breasts.
I stared at the godly sight,
　　and could not hold
　　　the moans and sighs.
"Who the hell was that fat guy,
　　who was with her
　　　the last night?"
What possibly could be the price
　　for such heavenly delight?
I would sell all that I had,
　　and even go
　　　to steal more money,

Just to smell her filthy body
   and to kiss her dirty thighs.

I found her in the back bar
   late at that night
She read the question in my eyes
   and whispered the price to my ears–
It was too high!
I asked her for discount
   or a credit of some-kind
– "No deal!",
But she gave me a sexy wet kiss
   for going an extra mile.
(She was only a whore,
   after all)
She left me burning with desire
   so I picked her second dancer
And burned her lustful
   through the night.

Somewhere in Brazil
Love In Lonely World

No, don't send me your photos—
   real girls are never as nice
     as the illusionary ones do.
Real love is never as sweet,
   and real sky is never as blue
As the imaginations of them do ...

Real wives are far from
   what the men dream of
Real love is the one
     we keep in our hearts
And the best sex is actually
     a good sweet kiss.
The best poem is the one
   you dedicate to a girl
Whose name
   you can not tell
     to anyone.

I met a girl once
   in a dark corner of a bar,
     somewhere in wild Brazil.
It was at night, and she was so nice
   she kissed so ... so sweet ...
     with her little tongue moving
     around and around.

I kissed her back the same way
and she fainted in my arms
"Please ... don't stop!!!" —
she whispered and begged,
It was as spring flowers
asking for release
While breaking
through the new grass,
Somewhere in mountains,
in the wild Brazil.

We knew both, however,
that we should not do it
"All the way" then and there,
but we did not want to end
this kiss.
Nevertheless, soon it was too late
to think
We could not stop it anymore
... in that bar,
We were by then
too far gone ...
And we made love right there
in the dark, empty corner
of this lonely world ...
Among spring flowers
somewhere in mountains,
in faraway Brazil.

Next time I met this girl
was in the same bar
after one month
And she looked very,
... very different
From what I imagined
when we made love
in that dark corner
of the bar.
This time she was drunk and vulgar
and kissed some other guys too ...
She had, though, memory of
what we did together before,
But behaved as if nothing happened
at all.
I took it cool as well
and played it into a corner,
As if, nothing happened at all
in that lonely night
in the bar's dark corner
When we were in frenzy
and made love
like crazy.
Suddenly, though,
I heard my own heartbeat
when she left the bar,
This time
with the other guys,
not with me ...

In a dark, lonely corner,
  among spring flowers
    somewhere in mountains,
    in the wild Brazil.

No, don't send me your photos—
Real girls are never as nice
  as the illusionary ones do.
Real love is never as sweet,
  and real sky is never as blue
As the imaginations of them do.

Love in a Rio Pub

In a pub full of people,
  with lights on and
    waiters watching
These two were talking
  and then they were necking
He kissed her earlobe
  nibbled on it a little,
Moved down to her lips
  and kissed her hard
She blushed and flashed
  and sucked his tongue
He inhaled her aroma
  all over from her neck
    to the head

He touched her
  breast coping it
Harder and harder ...
  pressing on the nipple
Both breathing heavy
  with moaning sounds

Oh, she suddenly stopped
  —Not here—whispering—no ...,
He moved his embracing hug
  from her breasts and dropped
    his hand to her thighs
Stroking her legs,
  sliding his fingers
    under her skirt.

Soon it got too much for the pub ...
  they were trapped
Between the viewers
  and the waiters,
Everyone else was rather proper,
  not going as far
Just watching ...
  and drooling
Or making gestures
  of disgust
Inside themselves
  simply envying them.

With her skirt wrinkled
    and his tie aside
The shirt still unbuttoned
    they had to leave at the end.

They were tipsy
    and horny
Both wishing each other,
    but could not at the end
        overcome the stringent
Lovemaking rules.

They left and I watched
    as they walked
Into the dark streets ...
    where it was windy
        and cold
Cooling their desire
    for lovemaking,
Making them sane again.

The Bullfight Ring

Some like to watch
  bullfights in the ring
Some would rather fight
  and die in there
The photo-man would die
  to get a shot of them—
Those who defie the fear
  those who aren't afraid of death.

The real action is always sudden,
  unexpected and thrill laden,
Your eyes pop out,
  ready to jump out of their sockets
Your heart races,
  your pulse goes wild
The reason fails
  to keep you still.
Glued to the camera
  you become wild
As wild as animals
  and the gladiators
And you see yourself
  as the gladiator
Who goes to kill
  or to be himself killed.

You make a snap-shot
  Oh ... you just missed it.
The second shot ...
  ... die or get it right!
You jump into the ring ...
  ... and there you die.

Who Said Hemingway
Loved the Bullfights

It's 8am, July 7th in Pamplona.
Fire the canon!
The Corrida starts.
Release the bulls!
The Fiesta begins.
 The crowd screams and runs
    to their possible chance
       of the bulls deadly brush.
Death so exciting and thrilling
It's even dubbed
    a "Right of Passage"!
The thousands run,
    screaming from their lungs
The bulls and the men
    all in one mass.
The bulls are gaining,
    and your body runs
To the Corrida gates
    which Ernesto guards,
       he will let you pass.

Who said Hemingway
    loved the bullfights?
He was drawn to them,
    but deplored in his mind

He was helpless though
   in his fascination—
      enjoyed the End as inevitable—
Like a boxer in the ring,
   that is to be knocked-down,
Like a bleeding bull,
   that is run down ...
      ready to be killed.
And Ernesto remained
   a wounded, but proud bull
      who shot himself at the end
Rather than be disgraced
   by a nameless
      and faceless death.

II
From New York

Free Kisses in the Big Apple
The Glass and Iron Jungle

Strolling across the Apple,
　the glass and iron jungle,
Passing by the girls,
　never really hugged,
　　never really kissed
And myself in there
　who's been over-kissed,
　　and over-hugged
And still craving and missing,
　not sex—just to be loved.

Once I ran into a girl
　just standing at the street corner,
And holding a huge banner:
　"FREE KISSES"
Now,
　I've seen and heard
　　all kinds of crazy things
　　　about New York City,
But this was too much,
　even for me!
I might not even believed
　If I didn't see it
　　with my own eyes.

No question, I went for it—
  we both laughed,
    kissed and hugged,
      even twice.
Of course, I asked
  if I could see her again
She said:
  —"Sure, come tomorrow,
    and kiss me again."
I got home
  and thought of all whores
    that I met and paid,
and some I even made
  into my Muse—for pay.
Maybe the girl was just trying
  to break into that stuff?
Or maybe she was just missing
  the other stuff, called love?
    just like me!
I did go the next day
  for the kisses and hugs
And she kissed me
  and hugged—twice again.
The third day, though,
  the hugs didn't feel the same,
    as the day before,
      and the kisses now
        felt really cold.

But I needed them badly,
  so I went back for the hugs,
    again and again.
Until the day
  when once,
    she was no longer there—
    —she was gone!
I still returned to that corner,
  and came back again,
but she had probably moved
  not leaving an address,
    if she even had one.
(Or maybe I just dreamed about her)
No, no, my friends—
  I didn't go to look for the girl,
I truly knew the case was dead
  (Or, maybe, that was me
    who was dead?)
I went, though, and
  bought a brush with colors,
    to make a color banner:
  "FREE KISSES"
Went back to the same corner,
  where the girl used to stand
Who knows, she might see me
  and come back.

And left my shrink,
  with his sessions.

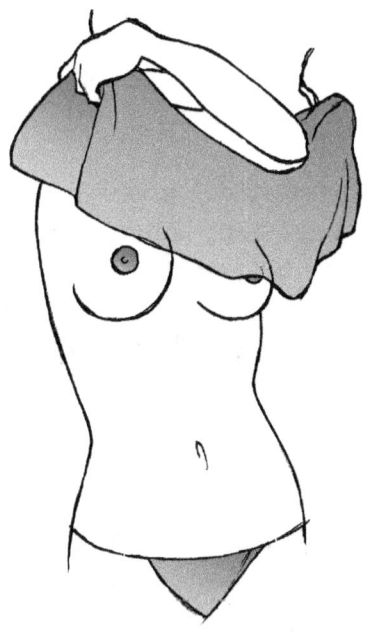

She Was Only a Girl
A Manhattan Girl

At first she entered
   the room like a flower
But she was a girl
   just a plain human,
Maybe a little scarred
   but still, only a girl.
I saw her nipples
   on her round breasts

Through the sheer shirt,
   that for the occasion
     she dressed.

She started to undress
   but I stopped her,
I wanted to watch
   her breast
They were pink and large
   with an oriole around them
Their aroma
   put me in daze a bit ...

I wished so to touch them
   to stroke and kiss
To hug and
   dive in them,
But she said
   to mind myself,
She was not here
   for that.

Trust me,
   it was so hard
To acknowledge that simple
   ... very simple truth
She was here not to be admired
   and even loved at all

She was not here to be adored
   for her breasts or nipples
She was here just for the sex
   plain, full service
   normal sex—
She was an escort girl.

... She was only a girl,
   a Manhattan Girl.

Sex for Shelter
Manhattan Ballad

It's 3:45 am at P. J. Clarke's.
Jerry just called the "Last Call" —
   the last drink before they close
Last song from the jukebox,
   and my last cigarette.

There were two girls
   sitting in the corner
Two ordinary girls.
The place was closing,
   but they did not look
      in any hurry at all,
         nursing the same glass
            for an hour now,
         chatting, whispering
         and laughing low.
They looked like people
   with no particular problems.
They were just girls —
   ordinary, everyday girls
      and nothing else at all.

Jerry brought them the bill
   and asked if they found
      what they were looking for.

The girls said all was fine
   there was nothing to worry at all.

P. J. Clarke's—the place where
   Frank Sinatra had
     his chosen seat.
     where Marilyn Monroe had
      her secret meetings and
   Louis Armstrong played
     his trumpet in the back room.
There were Johnny Depp,
   Jack Nicholson, and many others too.
The 19th century relic of New York City
   living its slow days now.
On the sidewalk,
I was struggling to zip my jacket.
   The girls walked out and stared.
I wasn't steady and
   my hat fell down.
     It was snowy
      and quite dumpy there.
The smaller girl picked it up
   and handed back to me.
I was drunk
   and they asked where I lived.
It wasn't far,
   so they offered to walk me.
There is my building,
   a luxury eastside building.

The doorman rushing
    to greet me, and
        to take me in his arms
            —away from girls.
The girls stopped,
    looking quite shocked—
        for sure they got scared
            of the doorman.

They were just girls,
    ordinary, everyday girls.

I invited them up for a night cap.
    The two kept staring
        till the older one nodded
            —Ok.

The Doorman bowed
    and opened the door.
The Hallman ran and
    called the elevator.
The elevator came
    with the Elevator man.
So, the girls and I loaded in
    with the Elevator man.
He pushed the floor button.

Once in the flat
    I opened the fridge—
        and my soul—to them.

Spoke of bad marriages,
   gold-diggers that sucked the blood
Floating islands and fine bars,
   young girls that gave me the jump
The fighting fields,
   where no rules were barred.

And then I noticed—
   the girls didn't talk at all,
I, actually, had no idea
   who they were, after all.
I looked at them—
   one was blond and tall
     with blue eyes,
The small one was auburn
   with brown eyes.
She was cute and charming
   with a mischievous smile.
The tall one had hips that moved
   like Marilyn Monroe's.
Her nose was tipped up
   like those Russian models.
She seemed more serious
   and kin of taking care of
     the younger one.
The cute one listened to her
   in return.
Both stared at me and listened
   like kids
     in kindergarten.

And here I was—a smart guy,
  like the professor.

So I asked
  what they were up to
    for tonight.

The tall one answered,
  after a pause—
"We are heading to Grand Central
  to take a train back to work."
"And when is your train?"
  "Tomorrow, afternoon"

I probably looked funny—
"And where are you sleeping,
  tonight?"

The tall one smiled with
  the charmer's smile, while
    the smaller one
      had fallen asleep

She poured another glass,
  for her and me,
    and gave a mischievous,
      sexy look to me.
"Well you could sleep here,
  I guess."—I said
    hardly hearing myself.

She touched my hand,
  leaned to me,
    and patted my
      graying hair—
"You are a real nice man,
  good man for the girls,
and girls will never forget it."

The morning broke in
  with a huge hangover and
    all the horrible attributes of it—
like a big headache, drinker's guilt,
  and the urge to repent.
One thing what wasn't clear to me—
  the reason, for what to repent!
And how would anyone
  benefit from that!?
Then, I gave up,
  and opened my eyes.
    ... call it a shock or hallucination,
There were two girls sleeping
  next to me ...
    in my bed!!!
I was naked and looked like
  I had sex with them
    last night!
I admit—lately I've been up
  and drinking much,
    but have never been forgetful
      that much.

So I pinched myself hard,
　　but my senses were right so far—
　　　the girls were naked
　　　　and quite real,
　　　　　by far.
I remember last night ...
　　I made it to P. J. Clarke's.
Then ... I might've stayed till the end ...
　　in that bar.
But, who were these
　　two cute girls ...

Finally I had to accept the idea
　　that I probably brought them here,
　　　myself, from P. J. Clarke's.
My headache was killing me
　　when they finally woke-up.
　　　I just wished they would
　　　　soon be gone.
But instead, I offered them
　　to wash-up
　　　and have tea with me.
Finally I asked their names,
The one was called Katia.
The tall and sexy was Svetlana.
The small one then came
　　and handed
　　　a headache pill
　　　　to me.

Then they fixed breakfast,
    and at last,
        we all sat down
            for the meal.
Then they spoke:

"We are babysitters working upstate,
    in rich suburban houses.
We also live and eat there.
We have one day off a week
    but there is a catch—
        we can't stay there
            for the night off—
                we have to leave and let them be
    alone in their own home for the weekend.
So last night was that our
    'night-off' night".

I listened to it all
    with a deep hangover.
This didn't make
    any sense to me, but
they were just girls,
    ordinary,
        everyday girls.

There was no need
    for any more questions.
I just mixed Screwdrivers
    for them.

"We have no friends,
    to stay with.
In the suburbs you can't even
    walk in the streets—
        everyone drives a car
        and there are no sidewalks.
So, we come to the city—
    it's easier here
        to find a place to sleep."

I downed another beer.
    The headache yielded.
The girls chatted softly
    and drank their screwdrivers.
I mostly listened
    and poured vodka.
In an hour or two we all got warmer,
    cozier and looser

"And, where do you actually
    sleep in the city?"—I asked
They giggled and smiled,
    sad and silly—
"Last night was a real bad night,
    after 4am all New York bars are closing
So, we could only go
    to a 24 hour coffee shop
        and sit there till morning
    thanks, really, for inviting."

Then they made sandwiches for all.
    Beer Chasers were real good.
I put some music on.

"How do we find a place
    on a lucky night?"
Giggling and laughing got
    silly and gloomy
"We go to discos and bars,
    meet someone there
      and they invite us
        to their place,
To sleep with them ...
    in their beds."

I downed a double shot of Chaser
    to close the door
      and not to think at all
Not to think what I just heard of!

I had a daughter myself
    that visited rarely
Living far away,
    somewhere in L. A.
She was quite busy,
    studying at UCLA.

I offered the girls more meals
and Screwdriver refills.

They were just girls,
   charming and sexy,
      but still quite real,
         everyday girls.

Then they spoke of their lives
   back in their old country.
That they had
   children over there.
One for each. And an old
   mother and grandmother
      to support.
Fathers of children were mostly gone
   but periodically showed-up—
to grab "their share"
   of the money,
      that babysitters send back home
         from their work.
Well, I guess,
   the Babysitter means
      a lucrative job, back there.

I called for Chinese food and cigarettes,
   and have a Pep talk to the girls—
About the fact that I liked them,
   as good people, and that
They could come back
   and sleep here anytime
      on their "night-off".

and that I wouldn't
   demand in return
      anything at all.
... And about the very strong Ego
   they must really have.

They said they didn't know
   what an Ego was
      but appreciated my offer
         and all that nice talk.

The doorman called on the intercom—
   "Delivery"
"Hey, food's here!"
Suddenly we all
Brightened up and smiled—
   there was a light, after all,
      at the end of the long tunnel.

I changed the tune to dancing.
The girls stayed till the night.
They sang and danced with swinging,
   filling this luxurious, empty place
      with music and laughing.

At the end
   we all took a joy ride—
      a cab ride through the city,
         to Grand Central—
            to the train.

"Good-bye my beauties,
    see you soon!"
Katia so cute,
    Svetlana so sexy.
They gave me a good-bye kiss,
    a wet one,
        and very sexy.

So,
they were not ordinary,
    everyday ...
they were real magic,
    after all!

I walked slowly to my luxury
    upper east side building.
The little girls were riding now
    the metro train to Westchester
    and probably napping
        or giggling low.
Girls, the magic girls,
    must sleep with any man
        (or a woman, for that sake)
Who would give them
    shelter for a night,
        a bed to crash on.

What would I do, however,
    if I was stuck at night
        with no place to go to sleep?

Would I sleep with anyone
    just for a bed to crash on!
Well, probably not with any (!)
    (I just couldn't perform with any)
But again, who's to judge,
    what could happen
        by cold night?

Besides that the girls and I
    probably share a similar fate—

They live in a luxury house
    and I live in a luxury house.
But neither of us
    has a real sweet home.
We are lonely, all.
Even though I have it All
    while they don't.

Then there are some differences too—
    the girls have the love of their family,
Have the kids,
    who depend on them,
And of course—the cause,
    to struggle for.

And, on the other hand,
    there are so many like me—

the decent, correct men
who have it almost all,
but no love at all.
And not even a cause
to struggle for.
The men,
who quietly crave for love
Any kind of love—
even a paid, or
a faked one.
Love for a night, for an hour,
or just for a while or so ...
Their cause could as well be, at least
helping girls with some money
to struggle for their cause.

Well, I guess,
the life is fair.
After all, it's not so bad—
money of these men
In exchange
for the girls' love and care.

You see, the world has the deal
after all,
nice and square deal.
And we all are
part of that deal too.

Just don't be two-faced,
   don't deny it
Or you might look
   the worse of us all.

The thought made me mutter
   sad and gloomy.
Am I a bastard looking for an alibi?
   probably yes,
     or maybe not?
Or, does it really matter
   after all?
Nothing is going to change
   an established order of the world
It's a done deal—
   an ancient deal

I entered P. J. Clarke's,
   cloud disappeared.
Jerry fixed me my first drink
   and put on my favorite song.
The smell of the old bar,
   and all the booze there was,
     brought me back to the earth
      and to the reality, as it was.
Girls will surely come back next week
   and I will take good care of them.

I'll be good to them ...
    ... and they will be nice to me.
After all, they are no ordinary
    everyday girls—
they are just magic,
they are my sweetheart girls.

On NYC Racetrack

A university professor,
  a reasonably sane New Yorker,
Went to a racetrack, incidentally,
  and won some money, accidentally.
He could have spent this money
  on his family,
    or going on vacation with his wife

Or to help his aging parents.
  but, suddenly he had second thoughts
He spotted that bitch,
  flashing her thighs in a mini skirt.
Brushing closely all the winners,
  like a scavenger,
    preying on rich ones.
He really fell for those cheek bones,
  high-heeled legs and her round ass.
He was a smart man though, and he knew
  the beauty was
    a whore and gold-digger.
He could not help it though—
  the money he had was free
He was not supposed to be there,
  to begin with.
So he decided to spend it
  on an illicit act,
    and do it quickly.
Then go back to his wife
  and act as if nothing happened,
    he had never been to any racetrack.
While he was thinking of clever reasons
  the blonde beauty was already there.
She sat next to him, crossing her legs
  making her skirt run up to her hips.
He could not resist, staring at stocking tops,
  garter belt hooks and that strip of white flesh ...
    stared at her blue eyes, eyelashes a flash.

He followed her in a sweet daze
    not even caring where it's going to end.
Then he was in a car,
    touching her thighs, up to the skirt.
        kissing and pushing up to her crotch.
Brushing her breasts, nibbling her nipples,
    smelling her fragrance and her woman's scent.
Next thing he remembers
    is running out of breath
        with her in bed.
Acting like a bad boy,
    smelling all over her body.

The rest of it was like in a movie:

He woke up, his wallet gone,
    but not his wristwatch—
        an unworthy piece of junk.
What remained was the smell,
    that smell of hers
        and the smell of sex.
There were also
    her tiny red panties
        which he held to his nose
He got dressed,
    his clothes cast about
Good thing his wife
    will never know about
        this trip and his whereabouts.

Then he smiled deep inside
As his wife will never learn about
all the future trips either.
About the bitchy, bloody beauties
with their long, high heeled legs,
"ladies" in short, micro-mini skirts.
As if a new man just awoke in him
(a man, not just a professor)
to condemned the old one
and start a new life.
He will come home and take a shower
so his wife will never smell
his spicy dirty smell,
Not a smell of sweat,
but the real smell of sex.
The smell ...
The smell ...
The smell ...

Wendy, Curly and Leggy
In the Woods of New York Upstate

To My Friend Lenny

Once upon a good time
of my proper lifetime,
I was a member of
an upper middle class
country club.

There were bungalows and club houses
    with a lake and a pool
        on one side.
All of it in the glamorous woods
    of New York, upstate.
The members were all good citizens,
    cheating on taxes,
        just within the proper limits
There was one black sheep though, a writer
    who worked downtown
        as a waiter among the low-life.
            He didn't pay any taxes at all.
Multiple divorces, booze, grass
    and young girls
        were his specialties over there.
As a writer he did not excel at all,
    but his girls were sexy and real,
        and they got younger as he got older.
He was street-smart, and good looking too,
    so there were, after all,
        things to envy him for.
Then there was Wendy,
    with curly hair,
        and a curvy body.
He just picked her up
    from his bar
        and brought her here for playtime.
To make a long story short
    Saturday meant party time
        at the swimming pool-side

Wendy got boozed
  and her swimsuit got loose.
Spoke of a back-ache
  and itching down there,
    in lower places.

The waiter was busy with the booze
  and couldn't take care of
    Wendy's ache
So I offered my doctor's hand
  to take care of
    her aching back.
"Ok, let's try it!" she said,
  and bent over
    the side of the chair.
"Yeah baby, let it be!"—I downed a shot,
  and facing the bunch of
    proper drooling eyes,
I massaged her
  from neck to waist
    yielding loud moans and sighs.
Running my hands to the south side,
  her sounds got wild—
    I drove her close to panting.
The writer watched it for a while
  and walked away
    in front of her eyes.
Like a dog, she followed him
  and for an hour to follow
    screams came from his bungalow.

All the honest and good citizens,
    just properly cheating
        on their taxes,
kept looking away,
    as if they did not hear
        anything at all.
The screams though, got
    louder and more rhythmic,
        decibels going up and down.
The party sounds and the music
    were overtaken soon
        by desperate screams for all.
Town cops did not arrive soon
    even the neighbors repeatedly called
As they knocked on the bungalow
    Wendy was screaming:
        "You are killing me ... no please ...
            I can't take it anymore!"

The cops banged:
    "Police! Open the door!!!"
"No, don't stop, please!" begged Wendy loudly.
    The writer yelled at the cops:
        "Go away!"
The cops instantly
    broke the door down,
        and found the waiter
Doing Wendy's royal bottom
    in a wild, but
        fashionable way.

The writer-waiter got later,
fired from his bar,
and couldn't take care of
his curly Wendy.
So, I sobered up,
went downtown,
and bought Wendy
a sweet candy.

Looking for a Place in New York

... In Someone's Heart

All you really want
  is to look for love
The love you lost
  when you grew-up
    and had to leave your mom.
Then you study and try to find
  money and a profi-job.
As you grow some more
  You start to look
    for another soul—
You want to find a mate.
But you suddenly find
  a brave-new world—
No one wants to take care of others,
  No washing, or cooking for them.
The men and the women
  They all want to work,
    have jobs, and make money,
All by themselves.
Seems like no-one cares
  for lost love, anymore.

As in a dense fog
  walking through the streets
Passing so close
  but not seeing each-other.

Then the rain starts
   and we all run for cover
Finding a shelter
   in a city corner
Standing so close,
   looking at each-other
Looking for a place
   in someone's heart...

In New York
   not somewhere else.

To Our Sons

Who Will Love Instead of Us

There is a time to come
There is a time to go
There is a time to love
There is a time to mourn

There was a high noon for us
There is the noon for them now
Our sons who'll live
   in place of us
And others, who'll love
   instead of us.

"People"—a Bunch
of Frightened Individuals

People are constantly hiding
Hiding behind each other,
   hiding in their past
    or even in their future.
Hiding behind the diplomas
Behind their wives
   or their husbands
Or even behind ...
   the musical instruments.
It's hard I guess
   to be in here, in the present
    and to be yourself.
It's scary and painful
   to face each-other
And even scarier
   to face yourself
    and your own fears.
People—a bunch of
   frightened individuals
    scared of life and each-other
Frightened of
   the mortals' reality
Choosing to pretend
   they are something
    or somebody else.

Looks like they are
   scared of themselves most.
Themselves,
   as separate individuals
      not just part of a crowd.

III
From Harlem

Be Strong or Die in Harlem
To My Friend Vlado Osif, a Painter

Harlem is a colorful world,
   perhaps the most colorful of all.
Harlem is the reflection of life itself
   with all of its most basic stuff.
Harlem is the challenge for survival.
A place where you either die
   or become stronger.

A French painter, Paul French,
   came from Montmartre-Paris
      to Harlem, New York City.
Leaving behind all the artsy people,
   All galleries and museums like Dorsey.
Paul also left his wife behind,
   who kicked him out, actually—
He wasn't making any money,
   his paintings were not selling.
She was always dressed like a classy lady
   and got tired of waiting
      for his talent to grow
         into some real money.
She first cheated on him secretly
   and later in public, as well.

Now in Harlem,
   he first had to absorb the shock.

He never saw so many people of different colors
  in the same place at once.
The faces were so diverse—
  some scary or full of rage,
  some even with humility or full of mercy.
He rented the cheapest flat,
  set one of the rooms as a painting studio
  and bought paint-brushes and paint.
Only then, by the way, he noticed
  that he was not alone, in there.
There were roaches, mice
  and even rats around.
He never ever saw anything like this,
  never knew anything like an anti-
  roach spray.
Never heard that cats eat the mice and
  that makes them people's friends,
  more so, than the mice.
On top of it all, the painter
  didn't speak much English either.
Here he was getting really desperate:
  he couldn't possibly paint his sunflowers
  while mice were running over his canvas.
He stopped sleeping at night—
  what if mice crawled inside ...
On the 3rd day, he banged his head against the wall
  and that turned out to be
  the luckiest thing for him—

The neighbor that he disturbed,
　was a young black girl, Laura,
　　from Haiti, who spoke French.
She got him the roach spray
　and rented him a cat, to eat the mice.

She looked about eighteen, to him.
He tried to paint his usual bright stuff—
children, flowers, and sky with the sun.
But it didn't work—
　the reality was rough and different
　　from what he used to paint,
　　　he felt alien to all this
　　　　and his paintings were missing a soul.
He went down the street to the alley.
　There was an abandoned lot
　　with junked cars.
The place was dirty
　with garbage all over.
Still this was best place for breathing fresh air
　and the best place to walk unnoticed.
That didn't work either, for long—
　he was seen and mugged at knifepoint.
So, he stopped going to the alley.
He was just sitting and staring at the
　canvas, couldn't touch the brush or
　　the paints.
His friends from Paris
　seemed long forgotten,

Since he left them
and moved to Harlem.
Then suicide came to his mind
as a right solution,
but, then—how does one do it?
He went at night to the window
of his second floor flat,
looked down at the street that was empty,
and thought of jumping—with his head down.
this may actually work, he thought.
At that very crazy moment
he saw the little Haitian girl, Laura.
She was in trouble—a couple of dark rough guys
ganged up on her,
groping and pushing her skirt up.
Paul, the French painter at first got scared,
froze and felt like in a maze.
Laura was fighting with all her legs and hands,
kicking and hitting them all over,
screaming in agony for survival.
The artist couldn't later recall
how he decided to jump.
To jump not with his head down,
but to jump upright and fight.
He saw the blood flooding his eyes
when he spotted an iron stick.
Paul didn't push or wrestle with anyone
he just swung, twice only ...
Next, on the sidewalk

there were two bodies,
  two bleeding heads with closed eyes.
Laura was pushing him back to the house
  telling him he must run now,
    that she will say—she swung twice,
    in self-defense.
Paul finally stepped inside
  before the police sirens
  blasted the streets.
He saved the girl
  and himself lucked out—
The rapists-thugs survived
  with only the broken skulls.
Laura told Paul the next day
  that their friends are after him,
    but not knowing so far,
      where to look.
From that day on,
  believe it or not,
    Paul didn't even consider
    Jumping out the window.
Suicide was no longer needed—
  he stayed in his flat, waiting for death
    to come through the door
    and get him.
Like a man on a death roll,
  or waiting for a guillotine,
    he thought of the life he lived,
      remembering all things
        that had passed.

All the colors and paintings,
   even his wife and her fits;
All the art galleries and even
   a gallery-man, Gerard,
     who rejected him and laughed.
He then started to paint in despair,
   just to fill the void,
     while waiting
       for his own death to come.
He also started to make love,
   to Laura,
So she would become, for him,
   his last sex
     and the last love.
The more sex he had,
   the more he wanted to paint.
He found himself falling in love
   with the canvas and the paints.
Laura brought food, cleaned and
   cooked;
     sometimes, she smoked grass,
      and passed a joint to him.
One day she looked at his new
   paintings, looked again and said:
"There is gonna be an exhibition, I've heard,
   of the Black Painters of Harlem, soon.
You could show your paintings there."
Paul laughed from all his lungs—

"Laura, do I look like a Black to you?"
"I may try to fix that. You just paint
and leave the rest up to me."
The time was running out, though—
the hospital will soon release
the rapists-tugs,
and they will come
to kill him.
What's gonna come first—his death
or artist's chance for glory.
And how is he gonna show up at
the "Black Artists" exhibition
while being so atrociously white!
The uncertainty fuelled the agony
and the agony fired his art of painting.
Each stroke of lovemaking
might be the last,
Each stroke of the brush
might, as well, be the last.
The canvas, full of his soul
was torched by the colors ...
and the race with time was on.
The day before the exhibition
things haven't changed much.
The good news—
he was still alive.
The bad news though,
he was still terribly white.
Laura had the cure:

"You know, I work at Tattoo
    and Body Painting shop."
She painted his whole body
    with a special paint
        which stays on for a day or two.
She gave him a fake ID
    with a black man's photo—
"You know, we all look alike"—
    she said—"And your name is now
        Malcolm Young."
By the morning, the French artist Paul
    was a new man—a man of color,
        a black man and a black artist—
            Malcolm Young.
You could have called him
    a Black or African American,
        he wouldn't really mind.
Finally, after all, the D-day has came,
    and here was the exhibition of
The Black Artists of Harlem
    in a nice little park just outside
        the Harlem Community Center.
And here came the public—visitors,
    even foreign ones, gallery-goers
        and the "Gallerists"—the real
            gallery-owners.
Mr. Malcolm Young with his exhibit
    of New Harlem Abstractionism,
        shining with his canvases,
            and with the young girlfriend of his.

Oh ..., oh my God! ... Who is that??!!
There was Gerard, from Paris, personally.
—Gerard, what brings you here, to
Harlem, he wanted to say,
    but Laura stopped him on time.
He was no longer Paul from Paris,
    He was now from Harlem,
        a Haitian-American artist.
Monsieur Gerard walked twice by Paul (Malcolm),
    looked at his paintings with a cold
        face, and politely introduced himself.
No, he didn't recognize Paul,
    just later he said that he reminded
        him of somebody else.
At the end, he bought Malcolm's
(Paul's) two paintings
    for the artist's discount, of course
        and gave him his gallery card,
Inviting him to stop by
    during his next visit in Paris.
The French boy
    gracefully accepted the invitation
        and then told Gerard that
He reminded him of one asshole
    from France, but surely he, monsieur
Gerard, couldn't be him!
Laura was ecstatic and ran off
    to help with the party, which has
        been set up to honor all the devoted
            art fans—

Blacks, reds, darks and lights,
   greens, yellows and whites ...
   and all the other possible colors.

       *   *   *

The Harlem folks at 125th and Lenox
   still talk about a French painter,
That painted his entire body black
   and won 1st prize
     amongst Harlem's black painters.
He was even invited
   to his own city of Paris,
     and went there as Malcolm Young—
      a black painter.
They say he still lives in Harlem
   with his young Haitian wife,
     as a black man himself.
But, I'll tell you man—
   Harlem is huge,
     and plenty of all kind of people
      live here,
And it ain't anybody's business
   what's the color of a black man
     once the Harlem is his address.
Inside we are all
   of all kinds of different colors.

Harlem is a colorful world,
  perhaps the most colorful of all.
Harlem is the reflection of life itself
  with all its most basic stuff.
Harlem is the challenge of survival.
  a place where you either die
    or become stronger.

$2 Deals In the Harlem Streets

I used to have $2 deals in the Harlem streets—
 that's coffee *and* The New York Times
  each for a dollar price.
I would sit on a broken bench,
 read it and drink my coffee,
And often even believed
 whatever I read.
It just seemed so correct
 to me.

Then I'd ride the A-train for just a buck
and Benny would meet me
at Dunkin' Donuts.
From there we'd go to Baba's Liqueurs—
to have a chat with local pals,
and get another $2 deal
on Harlem's moonshine.

Then we would sit in his place and
wait until Louise would come.
A fat black lady who had two daughters,
both ugly as hell.
Louise was fine though, herself.
She would complain of Con. Ed. bills
and not getting support for her kids
from their fathers.
Benny couldn't care less about her kids
and neither did I,
But we would listen to all her comlains
with very serious eyes.
Why?
There was a catch—
Louise was bringing us food.
(She worked at Harlem Diner.)
Finally we'd all get drunk
and she would sleep with Benny
(or me).

Those were good times on the Harlem streets.

Then Benny got early Alzheimer's
   and could not remember
      why we would wait for Louise.
As for me, I still remember, though
   even I forget
      what I had for breakfast.

Nowadays,
   I still get $2 deals on the Harlem streets—
      but now it's either coffee *or* The New York Times,
         each for two dollar price,
            and you pay two bucks for the trains.
Well, I skip the Times—
   one can hardly believe
      whatever they write.
And I don't ride the A train
   anymore—
Benny is gone
   and Louise moved out.
Two daughters of hers
   happily joined
The forces of NYPD,
   and then they
      also got married.

Now, I don't even remember
   why I started all this.
By the time anybody reads
   this sheet

There ain't probably be
  no $2 deals in the Harlem streets.
There may not even be
  coffee at Dunkin' Donuts,
Everyone would correctly drink
  coffee from Seattle at Starbucks
And the trains then
  will probably run
    for a whole
      three earnest bucks.

Nightly Harlem

Wandering through nights,
    the streets and homeless sights
I once met shabby girls
    with city junk at their sides.
They slept like babies
    among old cars with no lights.
Night was chilly with no one
    to look at this sight.

Harlem Riots

Imagine a world without tourists,
funny artists or psychotherapists.
In Harlem there is no need
for the shrinks,
Since the neighborhood
is a family for them.

There were riots in Harlem recently-
Screaming, yelling, fighting,
  rocks and bottles flying,
    and windows breaking.
Big fat ladies, more aggressive
  than their men who were
    tipsy or stoned ... a little.
In the chaos and confusion
  store owners closing doors
    and rolling down the shutters.
The reason for the brawl was insignificant
  and soon wasn't even relevant.
These were Independence Day
  fireworks that misfired
    (And also were illegal).
Once the crowd is worked up
  the Reason is gone.
Garbage cans get torched
  and people start to push
    each other.

Everyone is ready to jump
    one another ...
That's when the cops show up
    and things really start-up.
Now,
    everyone hates the intruders!
The policemen become their target,
    especially once they try
        to make an arrest.
Not waiting long,
    the crowd gangs up on them
        calling names, throwing rocks,
            and even hitting the "others".
The excitement grows, and
    everyone feels a part,
        of his own neighborhood.
They have to stick together
    like a family,
        to resist aliens—the cops.
Fight and work together,
    against the intruders,
      who don't belong here.
And there is a feeling
    of the high flying Freedom—
        when you can literally
           push the cops.
It's like pushing the state
    and the authorities.

You feel free and moreover,
   you've earned that Freedom!
The cops—NYPD centurions
   retreat at last.
Leaving behind yelling, laughing
   and victorious crowd.

In Harlem there is no need
   for psychotherapists—
The Neighborhood is their cure
   and their family therapy.

Blond Courtesan in a Harlem Club

To sit in the Lenox Jazz Club
  is a good thing to do in Harlem.
No, it's not only the jazz,
  There you meet all kinds of gals.
Once I sat there
  with an old friend of mine,
When a new gal walked in,
  who I had never laid my eyes on.
She eyed the place in and out.
  The lady was leggy, white and blonde.
Dressed in a sheer blouse
  with the deepest cleavage,
    she was also all alone.
She sat on a high chair by the bar
  ordered Black & White and glanced around.
Shortly after the gal got up,
  with high heels and round ass
    wrapped in short white skirt,
She walked slowly, swaying her hips,
  moving toward a sign—
    "Ladies" and "Gents".
A new working gal?
  a blonde beauty here,
    in the black Harlem?
—Gotta check her out.
  I ordered her another round
    which she expected.

—"So what's the deal? What's your name?"
—"Blondie is my name,"—she said.
—"How come you're not in the fancy Chelsea
  or at least in Astoria Queens?"
She glances at me and I understood
"Ah ... I see,
  the competition there is too high".

As the real estate prices move up,
  the ladies dress hemlines
    follow them up.
And the gals move up,
  "up", from downtown.
—"How much is the going rate, if I may ...?
  Oh ... no, that's way too high!"
    —I exclaimed as she answered.
—"You'll be surprised,
  just wait and see
    with your own eyes"
You wouldn't believe it,
  but she was right.
The black gentlemen in tuxedos and ties,
  the Nouveau Riche of Harlem, you know
Those that frequent the fancy jazz clubs
  the music lovers ..., I mean.
In no time she was taken
  Out with them and into the limo.
Came back later,
  and got taken again.

Sallie, the regular
working black girl,
Even for a lesser price,
didn't get lucky all night.
She asked me for a drink
and I paid for her meal as well.
Once Blondie returned
the third time now,
Sallie rolled her sleeves
and got real loud,
but it was too late already—
Blondie got a bodyguard,
standing next to her,
cool and trendy guy.
I took Sallie home that night.
She showed me her kids and cried—
She couldn't afford
to come home
empty-handed.
I hugged her, wiped her eyes,
and gave her some money.
I walked back to the Jazz Club,
looked up at the blonde gal,
and told her,
She shouldn't really bother
coming here any longer.
Sitting on the high bar chair,
she crossed-uncrossed her white legs,
the short hem of her white dress
lying on her sexy legs,

She looked at me
    with a glowing look
      and offered
        to be mine ...
          for free!
I contemplated for a minute and said,
    "Free wouldn't fly,
      but I could take care of you, say
        for 30 percent off your pay."
She responded in a business manner,
    saying it would infringe on her profit
      leaving her just a tiny margin,
    —"I already pay Larry, my white guy 40%,
      it's gonna be Peeling him
        unless I pay the Moving tax,
          I'm not a "Choosey-Suzie".
OK, I promised her to keep it in secret
    and we settled it for 10 %.
But with one simple condition—
    Blondie would stay away
      for at least 3 business days
So Sallie and her sisters
    could feed their kids
      and pay their pimps.
Here Blondie was all hearty smiles
She gently touched
    the black hair of mine
      and kissed me sexy
        on the black cheek.

Well, I thought,
  Blondie probably
    was worthier of her price,
So I took her deep discount
  bought her candy,
    and took her home.

Farewell

Georgian Poem

ავთანდილ პაპიაშვილი
გამოთხოვება

ნახვამდის მთებო, ბუმბერაზებო,
ნახვამდის ჩემო თეთრკალთიანნო,
ნახვამდის თერგო, გიჟო არაგვო,
მივდივარ, გტოვებ ჩემო სამშობლოვ.

უკან დავტოვებ უღელტეხილსა,
თვალთაგან გაჰქრება მშფოთვარე ხევი,
ვეღარა გნახავ დათოვლილ მთებსა
მე იქ დამხვდება ტიალი ველი.

ჩემო ძმობილნო არაგვო, თერგო,
ვეღარა გნახავთ თქვენ კიდევ დიდხანს
დამემშვიდობეთ, გადამეხვიეთ,
მითხარით რამე განშორებისას.

იცოდეთ თქვენგან მოცილებულ კაცს,
გაშლილი ველი ევიწროვება,
ხშირად გასცქერის ზეცის კიდესა,
მაგრამ ვერ ჰხედავს იქ მთის კალთებსა.

მაგრამ კაცნი ვართ ჩვენ ამ ქვეყნისა,
დაღონება კი არ ჰშვენის კაცსა,
ნაღველს გავაქრობთ, იმედს ვახარებთ,
დაბრუნებისა შევსვათ ფიალას.

Farewell
Translation from Georgian

Goodbye my giant mountains
with your white snowy peaks
and steep mountain proud rivers
named Aragvi and Tergi.

I am leaving mountain gap behind,
never more will I see the raging springs
in the place where I am heading to,
a wretched prairie awaits for me.

My dear brothers Aragvi and Tergi,
I will not see you for the longest time,
please embrace me now and
wish me luck on my long journey.

And please remember, the prairie is too
narrow for the one who has left you.
No matter how far I look
I won't see the mountain-tops any more.

Yet, we are proud men of our land,
we shall not give way to sorrow, and
should hope for the best of fortune
and toast to our happy return.

About my writings

I started to write when I was twelve. It was a love letter written as a poem to a neighbor-girl. (All Georgians are poets a little.) The letter wound-up in the hands of her mother and she immediately destroyed it, since it could compromise the honor of her ten-year-old daughter. My first poem goes back to my sweet seventeen and is written in Georgian language. The rest of the poems I wrote in the next five years are in Russian—that is where I studied in medical school. I stopped writing for several years during my medical-psychiatric practice, but renewed it in a Refugee Camp outside of Vienna. There I wound-up as a political defector from the Soviet Union and Russian-occupied Czechoslovakia. I wrote a novel about my life as a Soviet psychiatrist, but never published it. This one was in Czech language followed later by number of Czech short stories that were lost before publishing. The same happened to some of my writings when I was a Manhattan "shrink". I wrote and published clinical-research studies during my "shrink" years, but I do not count them here.

Finally the "miracle" happened—I fell in love (again) in Paris and it was like being seventeen again—as if big water broke a dam and swept me into a madness of writing a poetry. Those poems are presented in my first English-language book—the one you are reading right now. The book is translated and published into Czech, Russian, and now in Spanish and Polish)

However, my first-first book has been a collection of my early Russian poetry called "Love Me Madly", but they are not yet translated into English. It is a Russian language book.

The first English language book "Courtesan and a Psychoanalyst" / "Free Kisses" (translated already into Czech, Russian, and in Spanish) contains a novelette of the same name, poems that are rhymed short stories, and a poem-essay about a KGB agent Ernest Hemingway (yes, I mean the Hemingway).

The poems in this book were written starting in 2007 and I dedicated them to those who inspire the poetry—"The Girls I Loved".

The issues of prostitution, Feminism, and sexuality are discussed in my philosophical comedy "Dracula's Brides for Hire"—my second book, which is scheduled for publication by the end of 2010. In this play-novel, Dr. Victor Frankenstein is a psychiatrist of Count Dracula in his Transylvania castle. He gets sexually involved with Dracula's three brides while conducting psychotherapy. They all later escape fearing Dracula's retribution and the USA grants them political asylum—as to the victims of Dracula's sexual intolerance. Subsequently, the brides become New York "high-class" prostitutes with Dr. Frankenstein being their pimp—he calls it a "Rent-a-bride agency." Director of FBI J. Edgar Hoover nabs their "agency" and the brides have to work for the FBI as well. Posing as classy call girls, they wire-tap KGB spies. Soon the famous American feminists and mobsters get on-board and a shootout begins. It lasts until Count Dracula himself appears and puts all in proper order. Afterwards, Dr. Frankenstein and the brides are send to Prague by FBI to find a nonexistent "American agent" Cimrman. Frankenstein is locked-up in a madhouse, but the girls liberate him seducing his psychiatrist. Later they find themselves entangled in a web of corrupted politicians, mafia and the KGB. Dracula intervenes again and saves his brides. Finally, they all meet the American young "metro-sexual" president together with the brutal Russian prime minister. The comedy is colorfully illustrated by an American artist T.M. Larsen.

A book after that is going to be a collection of my American short stories. These are from Harlem ("Don't Fall in Love with Choosey-Suzy", "Beyond any Fear of Dying"), Queens-Upstate N.Y. ("Whatever he doesn't know can't hurt him"), Las Vegas ("Eye for an Eye"), and from the Caribbean Islands ("Diary of a Sexual Tourist"). What are the short stories about?—Mobs, cops, workin' gals, cheating spouses and pedophile priests. They are also about love and courage in times of AIDS.